Caught!

Books by
Willo Davis Roberts

Caught!

Willo Davis Roberts

A JEAN KARL BOOK

Atheneum 1994 New York
Maxwell Macmillan Canada
Toronto
Maxwell Macmillan International
New York Oxford Singapore Sydney

To my granddaughter Sarah
—WDR

Atheneum
Macmillan Publishing Company
866 Third Avenue
New York, NY 10022

Maxwell Macmillan Canada, Inc.
1200 Eglinton Avenue East
Suite 200
Don Mills, Ontario M3C 3N1

Macmillan Publishing Company is part of
the Maxwell Communication Group of Companies.

First edition
Printed in the United States of America
10 9 8 7 6 5 4 3 2 1
The text of this book is set in 12 pt Palatino.

Library of Congress Cataloging-in-Publication Data
Roberts, Willo Davis.
Caught! / Willo Davis Roberts. — 1st ed.
p. cm.
"A Jean Karl book."
Summary: After a bus journey in search of their father, thirteen-year-old
Vickie and her younger sister discover that he is missing and may need
their help.
ISBN 0–689–31903–7
[1. Mystery and detective stories.] I. Title.
PZ7.R54465Cau1994
[Fic]—dc20   93-14422

1

I'd had a reputation for being crazy ever since I let Sean Wilson and Hank Kavorkian talk me into going wild river rafting with them down the Stilly. That was almost two years ago, right after my eleventh birthday, but it's hard to live down a thing like that. Especially if you have someone around, like Gram, who never figured out that forgiving and forgetting are supposed to be virtues. Of course I was never her favorite granddaughter in the first place.

It didn't seem crazy at the time. Hank borrowed his dad's rubber raft—I didn't know until later that he didn't have permission—and we took some sandwiches and a net bag full of pop cans we dragged behind us in the river to keep cold.

The water was low, which we thought would make it safer than in the spring, when it had been so high. How could we have known that meant the rocks would be more likely to stick up high enough to puncture the raft?

We were wearing life jackets, and the search-and-rescue team commended us for *that*. At least nobody drowned, though I swallowed a whole lot of water when we first went under. The pop cans weren't the only things that were icy cold by the time we waded ashore.

And then we found out we weren't on the main bank but on a little tiny island, and the current was too swift for us to get back where we belonged. Sean made a try, but we didn't have any ropes or anything, and when he got out to his armpits and then was knocked off his feet, we were lucky to be able to grab him before he got carried downstream. He did cut his forehead on a rock when he fell. I'd never realized how bad it looks when you bleed into water and it leaks all over you.

I knew right then, sitting on the bank, that we'd been stupid. The raft was gone—Mr. Kavorkian was going to have a fit about that—and our lunch and our pop were gone, and we were stuck on this island for the night. Our clothes eventually dried out, but we didn't have any jackets, and it got pretty cold before dawn.

I didn't need a lecture when I got home. I mean, by that time I had figured out for myself that we hadn't been totally smart. The search-and-rescue guys were nice, but they pointed out that we could have been killed. And then when Mom and Dad met us after we'd been airlifted off the island by helicopter, they said they'd been worried that we'd all drowned when we capsized. So it wasn't as if it was news to me that maybe white water rafting with a couple of guys who didn't know much more about it than I did was dangerous.

But leave it to Gram, she had to say all of it again,

plus putting in her two cents worth on how wild and crazy and unladylike I was. And how it was about time I learned to *think* before I acted.

Actually, I usually did think before I acted, only just not for very long. So that's why I did something else that might have turned out to be not only stupid but *fatal*, without my thinking too long about the possible consequences.

It wouldn't have happened if Mom hadn't gone off on a business trip for a week, though I guess that wasn't a good excuse. But she *knew* how I hated being left with Gram even for the few hours after school.

I was feeling okay when I walked in the door, but Gram started right in.

"Don't head back out the door, young lady," she said, looking up from the chicken she was preparing to stick in the oven. "Not until you've cleaned up your room."

"I'm working on a project with Margie," I said, plunking my books down on the table. "For science. I have to go over there to do it."

"Not until your room is clean," Gram said, giving me a look calculated to turn me into an icicle.

"It can wait until we get our project organized, can't it?" I demanded. "I mean, nothing's going to get any worse in the meantime."

"You've been told to clean that room every day for a week," Gram said, her mouth going flat the way it does when she isn't happy with me, which is practically all the time. "Now you're grounded until you do it."

"You can't ground me from schoolwork!" I protested.

"Don't tell me what I can do, Victoria Ann Rakosi," Gram warned. She always says our last name as if it's a swear word, as if there's something wrong with having a father whose family came from Hungary. "I am in charge while your mother is gone, and I say you'll clean up that room before you step outside this house."

I glared at her. I knew that if Mom were home I'd be allowed to work on my science project with Margie. But the way Gram was acting, I wouldn't have been surprised if she'd grabbed me by the hair and thrown me in my room and locked the door.

"And change your clothes first," Gram added.

I stomped off down the hall without answering. Tears stung my eyes as I slammed into my bedroom. It wasn't like this before Dad left. Gram lived in her own place then, and we only saw her on Sundays, mostly. And while she picked us to pieces every chance she got, she hadn't been around to do it all the time, the way she was now.

I missed Dad something awful.

I sat down on the edge of my rumpled bed and stared at the room. It wasn't that bad. Sure, the bed needed to be made, and there were some clothes to hang up and a few books scattered around. But it wasn't *dirty*.

Dad's picture stood on the nightstand between my bed and Joanie's. I picked it up and looked into his face. Smiling, loving. And gone. Way to heck and gone, gone. Not here in Marysville, Washington, but in San Sebastian, California. Over a thousand miles away.

I wished he'd let me go and live with him there.

4

"Honey, that won't work now," he'd said when I asked him. "And your mom and Joanie need you here."

"But I need *you*," I'd pleaded the last time I'd seen him. And he hugged me, and his voice got husky.

"I need you, too, Vic, but it's not in the cards now. Maybe one of these days."

One of these days I hoped he and Mom would get back together, but with Gram working against that I didn't know if it would ever happen. I knew Mom didn't hate him, the way Gram did. Mom never said a word against him, and sometimes she even spoke up and made Gram stop when she got on one of her tirades against him. According to Gram everything that ever went wrong in the whole world was Dad's fault.

I don't think he'd ever have left if it hadn't been for Gram. It was one of the reasons I couldn't stand her.

She stirred up trouble. Mostly she tried to make everybody think bad things about Dad, and it upset Mom when the two of them said nasty things to each other. The only real fight I ever heard between my parents was over Gram, and Mom cried, "She's my mother, Steve! I can't abandon her!"

And Dad yelled back, "Well, I can't stand having her in the middle of my life! So if it's a choice between us, you choose her, is that it?"

When Mom just stood there, looking pitiful, Dad walked out and slammed the door. I think he gave her a chance to change her mind, but Gram kept working on her, and even though I think she didn't really want him to leave, Mom felt guilty about "abandoning" Gram, as she put it, when Mom was her only child, and Gram had little money and health problems.

I didn't know what the problems were. They didn't stop her from grousing about everything. She didn't believe in suffering in silence, the way Mom did. And Dad was too stiff-necked to come back home without being invited, especially when Gram moved in almost as soon as he walked out the door.

I don't think Mom actually asked her to, but after Gram talked about how hard it was for her to make it alone on her Social Security, and how much help that money would be to keep up the payments on our house, Mom never quite got up the nerve to ask her to leave. And Dad sure wouldn't come home while Gram was there.

It was true that when he left he made it impossible for Mom to be able to afford to keep the house, especially after he lost his job. Gram made a big deal out of contributing her pension checks to keep us going.

It wasn't worth it, as far as I was concerned. Joanie and I had to move into the same bedroom, Dad wasn't part of the family anymore, and Gram moved in and became the resident grouch.

"Vic?"

My little sister's head popped around the corner of the door. "What's making Gram so crabby?"

"Me, as usual." I threw a pillow from my bed to hers and flopped backward. "I don't suppose you brought anything to eat with you. The atmosphere in the kitchen wasn't conducive to my making a sandwich."

Joanie was only nine, but she knew what *conducive* meant. It was a word Gram used a lot. As in "your behavior isn't conducive to a peaceful household, Victoria."

She came in and sank onto the opposite bed. "I've got an apple and three cookies," she said, and began to unload the pockets of her jeans.

I sat up. "Good. I get half the apple and two of the cookies."

She looked at me soberly. "Half the apple and one and a half cookies," she corrected.

"But I'm bigger. I need more."

Suddenly her dimples showed. Joanie's cute when she grins.

"Possession is nine-tenths of the law," she said.

It was what Dad used to say when we wanted something he had, and we'd wrestle him for it.

I took the little jackknife he'd given me and cut the apple in half. Joanie inspected the halves carefully before she chose one. I prided myself on being able to make them absolutely even, no matter what I divided.

Then I cut one of the cookies in half. They were chocolate chip and walnut, and they were delicious. I have to admit Gram can cook, even if she is a pain in every other way.

"Gram said you have to clean up your room," Joanie said through a mouthful of crumbs. "And that you're grounded."

"Only until the room's clean," I said, not trying to

cover my resentment. "Come on, it's half your room, now. Help me clean it up."

"But my bed's made and all my stuff's picked up," Joanie pointed out, not moving.

"So what? The next time you leave your toothbrush on the edge of the sink, I'll put it away for you."

"Big deal," Joanie said. "Your generosity is exceeded only by your good looks, Vic."

That was another one of Dad's sayings. It was almost more than I could stand. "Joanie, do you miss Dad something awful, too?"

"Quite a lot," she said, sobering again. "Especially when Mom's gone."

"Yeah. And she won't be back for a week. Why can't she have a job where she doesn't have to travel so much?"

"She could," Joanie said. "Only she makes more money on *this* job, remember?"

I remembered. I also remembered how it had been when Dad was here, and there'd been enough money to buy the groceries and make the house payments and still have some left over for fun things sometimes. These days I felt guilty if I even asked if we could afford to let me go to the movies with Margie. Especially if Gram barged into what was none of her business and said, "Why do you badger your mother for money when you know what a difficult time she's having financially, Victoria? In my day we didn't ask for movie money. We went out and earned our own."

How, though? I'd have been glad to earn my own, but Mrs. Hovland was the only one who'd let me baby-sit her kids, and she didn't go out often enough to enable me to earn very much. There weren't any other neighborhood jobs.

I picked up a damp towel and snapped it at Joanie. "Come on, help me pick up this place or I'll beat you up."

She stuffed the last of a cookie into her mouth. "Well, if you put it that way. But I expect a favor in return. I'll let you know when I decide what it will be."

We hauled clothes to the hamper in the laundry room, made the bed, threw things out of sight into the closet. The books were neatly stacked on the dresser. I crammed all the loose papers into the top desk drawer, and slid the Monopoly game out of sight under the bed. "There," I said. "I hope she's satisfied."

When we called her to look at it, she didn't say she wasn't. But naturally she didn't say we'd done a good job, either. Sometimes she did with Joanie, but never with me.

I wasn't sure why she liked Joanie better, but I figured maybe it had to do with our looks. Joanie's small and cute, with fair hair like Mom's. In fact, she looks just like the pictures of Mom at that age except that she has Dad's brown eyes. Apparently that isn't enough to get her on Gram's hate list.

And I, on the other hand, am practically Dad's spitting image. Dark hair that curls just a little, no dimples, but an attitude problem.

That's one of Gram's sayings. "You have an attitude problem, Victoria," she would say when I was only trying to be funny. And so, of course, did my father. Whatever he had thought about anything—and according to Gram he had a peculiar sense of humor—was a sign of his deplorable "attitude problem."

Mom used to say that she'd married him because when they met she thought he was like a gypsy, which he claimed his ancestors in Hungary had been, and that intrigued her. Gram was definitely not intrigued by gypsies or rogues of any kind. She hadn't wanted Mom to marry anyone named Stavo Rakosi in the first place—she decided that before she even met him, which shows you how bigoted she was—and she made it plain now that she was glad he was gone.

I knew Mom didn't share her opinions, but I wished she would speak up more firmly in Dad's defense when Gram criticized him. After all, my folks weren't divorced, just separated, so far, though Gram made it all too clear that she thought the marriage should be ended once and for all. Mom never argued with her, just listened to what her mother said without comment; but she hadn't filed for divorce, either. I prayed she never would.

Anyway, Gram didn't say anything when I announced I was going over to Margie's, except to tell me to be home for supper at six.

I meant to be. Only we ran into some problems, and by the time we got them cleared away, it was later than I thought. It was twenty after six when I walked into the house.

Joanie and Gram were almost finished with everything but dessert. The chicken, potatoes and gravy, and peas were all cold.

Gram didn't jump me, just looked grim. Joanie

shot me a glance that told me Gram had been jawing about me before I got there. I loaded up my plate and took it back to the kitchen to stick it in the microwave, then sat down in my usual place.

When I picked up my fork, Gram said, "We usually say grace in this household."

My head snapped around. "I said it silently, just to God," I told her. "I didn't realize *you* had to hear it." I knew it was rude, and Mom would have reprimanded me, but I just resented Gram so much I could hardly bear to sit at the same table with her. If it hadn't been for Joanie, I'm not sure I'd have even tried.

Gram's mouth just got flatter and tighter.

Joanie tried to lighten things up. "There's a letter, Vickie. From Dad."

"Really?" That actually did make me feel better. "What did he say?"

"We don't know. Nobody opened it," Joanie said.

"Well, where is it? Let's find out!"

"It's addressed to your mother," Gram said. "We don't open other people's mail, do we?"

"But Mom won't be home for a week! She wouldn't care if we opened it!"

"You can't possibly know that. You will not open it, Victoria."

Frustration flooded through me. "But she always shares Dad's letters with us."

"That's her privilege. It's not mine. You will leave the letter until she comes home."

I wanted to hit her. I wanted to cry. I wanted my dad so bad it hurt. Even seeing his handwriting would help some, I thought.

I pushed back my chair and stood up. "Then I'm going to call him."

"Sit down and finish your supper so the table can be cleared," Gram ordered. "It would be wonderful if for once you considered someone besides yourself, Victoria."

I swallowed the rage I felt and sat back down, but I didn't forget about calling Dad. He'd probably tell me to mind what Gram said, but I was betting he would say we could read the letter, too. He hadn't known Mom wasn't going to be there to open it right away.

It might have been all right even then if Gram had stopped there. But she didn't.

"It's time you admitted that your father doesn't want to be bothered with you. You're old enough to be realistic," she said.

"That's not true! He cares about us, he loves us!"

Her thin lips twisted. I wondered how she could look as much like Mom as she does and yet have none of Mom's kindness, her gentleness, or her fairness. "That's why the child-support check is late again. That's why he's behind on his payments. That's why he writes once every couple of months instead of regularly, once a week or so."

"He's busy working, you know that," I defended him hotly. "And he sends money when he can. And he calls. I hear Mom talking to him sometimes, late at night."

Something changed in her face, and I realized that she hadn't known about those late-night phone calls. She didn't want to hear about any communication between two people she hoped were going to get a divorce.

I bit my lip, sorry I'd revealed it, and hoped she wouldn't take it out on Mom once she came home.

"He cares," I said stubbornly.

"Stavo Rakosi is a selfish, irresponsible man," Gram stated in a way that defied me to refute it. "If he really cared, he would meet his obligations willingly, and on time. He wouldn't have left a wife with two children to support."

"He was out of work for a while, but he's trying to catch up!"

"He's the same as he's been all his life," Gram said, driving her anger deeper into my heart with the words. "And the sooner you accept that, the better off you'll be."

She rose and began to take dishes off the table. Joanie was huddled unhappily in her chair, and as soon as Gram went to the kitchen I spoke to her.

"He *does* care, Joanie. Don't listen to her. She never liked him."

"I know," Joanie said softly. "Why don't you call him, Vic?"

So I did, or tried to. Mom's address and telephone book was on the telephone table, and I looked up Dad's number. It rang and rang on the other end, but nobody answered.

My throat ached with the need to talk to him. But there was nothing more I could do.

Gram came through the dining room again on the way to the TV, where she was going to watch something educational, no doubt.

"I checked your room," she told me in that cold, hateful way. "You were supposed to clean it thoroughly."

"I did," I said, immediately on the defensive.

"You stuck some of your junk under the bed instead of putting it away."

"The Monopoly! I always keep it there, it doesn't fit anywhere else. Mom doesn't care."

"It would fit in the closet if you didn't have it so crammed full of trash. You never totally obey what I tell you, do you? Well, your little show of rebellion will have consequences this time, Victoria. You're grounded until your Mother comes home."

I couldn't believe she was doing this. If Mom had been home, she'd never have stood for it. Indignation flooded through me, and I opened my mouth to say something else rude, I suppose. I hadn't decided what. But she beat me to it.

The letter from Dad, with that familiar dashing handwriting that covered half the envelope, was lying beside the phone. Gram reached out and picked it up.

"I'll just keep this out of temptation's way," she said, and carried it into the living room.

I don't know if I'd have opened it against her orders or not. I only know that she made me furious.

Joanie followed me when I turned and went back to our room, and closed the door behind us.

"I hate her," I said. "I almost hate Mom for leaving us here with her."

Joanie's lower lip trembled, the way it did when she was upset. "She had to, Vickie. She has to work."

"I know it," I admitted. "Maybe she wouldn't

have to work so hard if she didn't have to take care of us."

It was the wrong thing to say. Joanie's lip quavered even more. "But then who would take care of us?"

And that was when the idea hit me. I admit I didn't think of the consequences any more than Gram said I usually did.

I felt my jaw grow firm as my teeth came together.

"I've had enough of sourpuss Gram," I announced. "I'm not taking any more of her."

Joanie's eyes grew round. "What are you going to do, then?"

My resolve firmed. "I'm going to run away," I said.

2

Joanie was looking at me as if I'd suddenly grown another eye in the middle of my forehead.

"Where are you going to go?" she demanded.

"To Dad's. Gram's wrong about him, he does love us. And he'll understand why I can't stay here this next week while Mom's gone. I *can't*, Joanie."

She licked her lips. "He's such a long ways away. How'll you get there?"

"On the bus. I'll crack the fat pig, and I'm pretty sure there's enough in there to buy a bus ticket. I've got a hundred-dollar bill in there that Grandpa Rakosi gave me, remember? And I haven't robbed the bank in a long time."

"You were saving it for Christmas presents," Joanie reminded.

"Well, that's a long way off, and maybe Dad'll be able to refund me the money for the bus ticket." I kept the pig under the bed, too, and Gram hadn't noticed him. I dug him out and began to pry the plug out of his belly.

He was a big pink china pig, and when I opened

him his contents spilled out onto my bed—nickels, dimes, quarters, and pennies—a few dollar bills— and the money Grandpa had given me.

I started putting the pennies back into the pig, and then I divided the rest into stacks of a dollar each. Halfway through, Joanie said, "I'm calling in the debt."

"What?" She'd made me lose my count, and I started over again with a handful of dimes.

"I said, you owe me for helping with the cleaning. I want to go with you. If you're going to California, I want to go, too."

"You can't," I said flatly. "You're too little."

"What difference does my size make? I'm not a baby. And you know how Gram will be. She'll be *so mad*, and she'll take it all out on me. You have to take me, too, Vickie."

It was true. When Gram was in a rage she took it out on anybody within reach. Dad was the only one who never let her do it, and I guessed that was one of the reasons he was gone now.

"I have some money, too," Joanie said, and stood up and got out her own bank. It was a clown that winked when you dropped coins into his wide mouth. She emptied it on her own bed and said, "Help me count it, Vic."

I drew a deep breath. Gram would be even madder if I took Joanie, but I could sure see why my sister didn't want to stay behind.

Mom would probably be mad, too.

The thought pricked me like a staple that had dropped into the carpet, when you stepped on it in your bare feet.

"Do you think Mom will punish us if we go?" Joanie asked.

"Probably. I don't care," I said recklessly. "It'll be worth it if we get to see Dad, and Mom wouldn't ground me for a whole week, I don't think. Even if she does, she'll treat me fairly while I'm stuck at home, which is more than Gram will do."

Joanie chewed on her lower lip. "I've never been grounded for a whole week," she said. "Even the time I used the spray Mom got for making garlic bread, when I thought it was the air freshener and it was just before the garden club came, she only grounded me for three days. I think it was three days for making the green slime, too. But never for a whole week."

"It'd be safer if you just stayed here, Joanie," I said. "You know how Gram'll be if she gets mad. She won't really do anything to *you* because she's mad at *me*."

She got a stubborn look. "If you're going to see Dad, so am I, Vic." She hesitated, then stated flatly, "If you don't take me, I'll tell."

"Don't be a brat," I told her. "That's blackmail, Joanie."

Her lower lip retracted, and she grinned. "Yeah."

I sighed. She'd probably do it, too.

"Nobody'll *kill* us, will they? They'll just be mad for a while."

"They'll be mad, all right. But not so much at you. It'll be my fault," I said, "because I'm older and it's my idea. Chances are nobody'll ground *you* at all."

"Are we going to pack suitcases to take with us?"

I gave her a look of scorn. "Of course, dummy.

What did you think, we're not going to change underwear until we get home?"

That made her giggle. "Are we going to leave a note for Mom?"

I considered. "No. There's too much to explain to do it in a note, and I don't trust Gram not to open it and read it. I'll leave a note on my pillow, though. For *her*. Saying we're leaving and we're okay and not to look for us, and we'll call after Mom gets home next week."

Joanie was sober again. "Do you think Gram will call the police?"

I shrugged. "By the time she finds out we're gone, we'll already be on the bus, and she won't know where to look for us. She won't think we'd go all the way to Dad's. She doesn't know about the money Grandpa Rakosi gave us." For just a minute my eyes stung again. "I wish *he* wasn't way back in New Jersey. I wish he and Grandma Rakosi were the ones who came to live with us."

Joanie nodded. "I wish Dad hadn't gone away."

"Me, too. But we're going to go see him, and there's no way Gram can stop us. You'll have to go out and tell her I'm mad and I've gone to bed to sulk. She'll believe that; she thinks I sulk all the time. And tell her you're going to take your bath and then read in bed for a while."

"I could tell her I'm going to bed because I feel sick," Joanie said helpfully.

"No, don't do that. She might come in later to check on you."

"We could roll up our sleeping bags to make it seem like we're in bed if she checks."

"Okay," I agreed, "we'll do that. We'll slide our suitcases under the beds once we get them packed, and I'll sneak out into Mom's room and call the bus station. I think there's a bus heading south about ten o'clock—remember, Dad took it once when his car was broke down?—so if we get the nine o'clock bus to Everett we'll make connections."

Joanie slid off the bed. "And I'll pack a lunch to take with us, okay?"

So we made our preparations, and waited until Gram was all absorbed in her TV program, and then we slipped out the front door and headed for Dad's.

I had no idea it would take so long to get to San Sebastian.

It was a good thing we brought sandwiches and apples and cookies, because it took us until the following night to get there. The bus stopped in just about every little town to pick up or let off passengers.

Joanie slept all night, and I did part of the time. It would have helped if I could have tilted my seat back all the way, but the man behind me gave me a dirty look and said it was going right in his face, so I had to put it partway back up.

Nobody asked us why a couple of kids were getting on a bus late in the evening—on a weeknight even—or where our folks were. Nobody spoke to us at all except an old lady with gray curly hair who asked where we were going.

I told her San Francisco. That was a big enough place so if they looked for us there, they wouldn't really expect to find us.

The lady smiled and said she was changing buses there, going on to Santa Monica, where she was going to visit her son. Then she sat across the aisle and went to sleep and snored.

Everybody else ignored us. There was a tiny little lavatory in the back of the bus, and we used it a couple of times, but mostly we just rode and thought, or at least *I* did.

I didn't change my mind about wanting to run away, but it did occur to me that maybe Mom would be more upset than I'd thought. Maybe she'd ground me for *more* than a week. But then I thought about how glad Dad would be to see us, and decided there was no point now in worrying about whether I'd be punished or not.

I remembered I should have called Margie and told her she'd better get another partner for the science project, but I didn't care about missing school. It was practically the end of the year, and my grades were good. So were Joanie's. I was pretty sure they wouldn't hold either of us back a grade because we'd missed a week or so.

Maybe, if we were lucky, Dad would decide we could stay with him and we wouldn't have to go back to school at all until the next fall, and maybe we could even go in San Sebastian.

I'd never been to the town where he lived now. He had been out of work for a few months right after he moved out of the house. Gram made it sound as if he were shiftless and didn't want to work, but that wasn't true.

He was an accountant for an electronics company, and they laid him off because the president had a new son-in-law he wanted to take into the business. It was only a matter of time, Dad said, before he found another position. Everybody needs accountants. He just had to keep checking around until he found a good firm that could offer him a permanent job.

And then a friend told him about an opening in California. I didn't want him to go, and he said he didn't want to be so far from us, either, but he thought he'd better take the job if they offered it to him, just in case nothing opened up closer to home. It turned out the first job had been only a temporary one, and he'd had a couple of other jobs filling in for someone who was sick or something, and a few weeks ago he'd moved to San Sebastian. He'd been in California nearly six months now, and it seemed six years.

As the bus hurtled through the darkness, I sort of dozed and thought about how it had been before, when we were all together. I thought about all the fun things we'd done. We always had fun, even when we weren't doing anything special, except on holidays when Gram came over.

I'd heard Mom and Dad joke about how she got married just to get out of Gram's house. Even Mom didn't get along with her all that well, because Gram kept telling her how she ought to do everything.

By the time Gram moved in with us, of course, Mom had lived away from her for years, and she didn't knuckle under to everything Gram said. But sometimes she did, over things she said weren't important.

I thought they were important. I didn't see why

Gram should have anything to say about what on TV Joanie and I watched, and how we kept our bedrooms, and what our allowances were. I didn't see why it should matter to her what kind of snacks we ate, or what time we got up on weekends, or if we played our own music in our room.

Life had been the pits since Gram came to live with us.

Well, even if Dad sent us back to Marysville, which I hoped he wouldn't, we'd at least have a good visit with him. I couldn't wait to have his arms around me in a big hug. I missed his hugs.

I wondered what San Sebastian was like, and what there would be to do there. I wished it was on the coast, near the ocean beaches, but it wasn't. Dad had said it got pretty hot there in the summer, not like in our part of Washington State. I decided it didn't matter all that much. Gram wouldn't be there.

We rode and rode and rode.

Joanie woke up very early in the morning. We each ate an apple, because the people behind us were talking about not being able to carry fruit into California unless you could prove you bought it in a supermarket so they knew it had been inspected. We didn't want to waste it. Then I took her back to the bathroom. There was hardly room for both of us to get into it at the same time.

"Are we almost there?" she asked when we got back to our seats.

"I don't know." The lady with the gray curls woke up, too, and I leaned across the aisle to speak to her. "Do you know where we are? Anywhere near San Francisco?"

"Heavens no," she said. "We're still in Oregon. It's a long way yet to San Francisco, even after we get into California."

So we rode and rode some more. We stopped at a place where a lot of the passengers went inside and ate breakfast, but Joanie and I stayed on the bus and had salami sandwiches.

Finally we saw a sign that said Welcome to California, and we stopped at a border inspection station where they asked if anybody was carrying any fruit. Nobody was. After that we kept going, and everything looked drier and drier—not green like it was farther north—and Joanie got squirmy and bored, and I entertained her with stories about what we'd probably do when we got to Dad's. Then I tried to remember all the stories I knew from books, and finally I gave up when she stuck her lower lip out and said she was tired of riding.

"Well, then you shouldn't have insisted on coming with me," I said a little crossly, pretty tired of riding myself. "You knew Dad lived a long way away."

"I didn't know it was going to take weeks to get there," she retorted.

It *seemed* like weeks. At one of the rest stops I got off the bus and got us each a cold drink and bought a bag of peanuts, but they were so expensive I decided we'd better not buy many treats before we got to Dad's or we'd arrive broke.

Actually, we ate all the food we'd brought with us before we finally heard the driver announce that we were there. "San Sebastian," he called out, and I was glad the lady across the aisle was asleep so she

24

wouldn't notice where we got off. Just in case anybody asked.

I stood up and dragged Joanie with me, with our carry-on bags. A few other people got off, too.

It was dark out when we climbed down from the bus. Most of the other passengers were being met by someone, and I sure wished Dad was there to meet us, but of course I hadn't been able to get him on the phone, so he didn't even know we were coming.

"I'm starving," Joanie announced as the driver hauled luggage out of the bay under the bus.

"Me, too. We'll eat as soon as we get to Dad's," I told her.

I had hated to spend the money for a cab, but I didn't know what else to do when I tried to phone him and nobody answered at his number. I hoped he'd be home by the time we got there.

San Sebastian isn't a really big town, probably only a little bigger than Marysville, but everything was unfamiliar. There were some sort of unusual people hanging around the bus station, and I felt uncomfortable asking any of them for help. Probably they were just homeless people, harmless ones, but there was no way to be sure about that, and some of the ones we walked closest to smelled bad. Joanie pulled away from them and squeezed up close to me. "I'm scared, Vickie," she whispered.

I was, too, a little. "It's okay," I said. "We'll be all right in a taxi."

The address was an old brick apartment house four stories high in a neighborhood of other old apartment houses. I paid the driver and turned to join my sister on the sidewalk.

"Well," I said cheerfully. "We're here."

Joanie was staring up at the lighted windows of the apartments. "I'm glad it wasn't close to the bus station. I didn't like the people there."

"Nothing to worry about now," I told her, not admitting how nervous I'd been myself. "We'll be with Dad in a few minutes."

"We're safe now," Joanie said, and I realized she'd really been quite scared.

"Safe," I echoed, picking up the biggest suitcase.

At least that was what we thought. Shows how wrong you can be.

3

It was still quite warm, even though it was fully dark. There was a little convenience store on a corner about a block away, and on the other side of the street a tavern called the Tenth Street Watering Hole. Its red neon sign made our skin look pinker than it really was.

There were a few people on the street, ordinary people who weren't scary at all, but I was still sort of nervous from the ones around the bus station.

A boy a year or two older than I was sat on the steps of the building, playing a harmonica. He glanced at us but kept on playing an old song Dad used to sing: "Red River Valley."

Then, just as we reached the door, the boy turned around and asked, "You need to find somebody?"

I glanced at him and decided I didn't like his looks all that much. He had long stringy hair, his shirt was torn on one shoulder, his jeans were so worn out Mom would have stuffed them in the rag bag, and he had the grubbiest athletic shoes I ever saw. "You need directions?" he asked.

"No, thanks," I told him, and reached for the door handle.

Please, Dad, I begged silently. Be here.

I don't know why it took that long for it to occur to me that he might *not* be here, or to wonder what we'd do if he wasn't home. Maybe Gram had one point, at least, when she said I didn't think things out ahead.

An old man came out of the apartment house and after he'd almost knocked me down he swore at the boy with the harmonica for being in the way. The boy lowered his instrument and said pleasantly, "Good evening to you, too, Mr. Becker."

The man had brushed against me as he passed, and my nervousness increased, though at least he didn't swear at *us*.

The door into the lobby wasn't locked. The bulb inside was so dim it was hard to see the names printed on the mailboxes at one side of the small entranceway.

"There it is," Joanie said, her eyes almost on the white card. It was Dad's printing: Steve Rakosi. 3B.

His real name, his gypsy name from the old country, was Stavo, but hardly anybody except Grandpa and Grandma called him that. From the time he was a little kid he told everybody his name was Steve, so he wouldn't sound so foreign. Other kids often make fun of foreigners, Dad told us, even though that's pretty stupid. "All those different names— Hungarian and Russian and Nigerian and Korean— they're what make America interesting," he said. "Everybody but the Indians who are native Americans came from somewhere else, and that's great.

But I like Steve for a first name. Nobody has to ask how to spell it."

I felt better, seeing it written out on the bit of white cardboard. "Three B," I said. "Come on, let's take the elevator. Hauling these suitcases, it'll be easier than the stairs."

It was the slowest elevator I ever rode in. And it strained to rise, as if it were old and tired and not quite up to the trip.

We got off on the third floor, where there was another bare bulb. The hallway was narrow, and there was an unfamiliar and faintly unpleasant smell, as if it had been closed up too long. A window at one end looked out on the street.

A door opened in one of the front apartments as we checked to see which one was B. A woman appeared in the crack of the light, a woman about Gram's age, with straggly white hair. She wore a flowered print dress, and she just stood there looking at us. The door she had opened had a 3A on it in tarnished letters, and behind her a dog was barking. "Shut up, George," the woman said, and the barking stopped.

I saw the B then on the door directly across the hall from her. I moved toward it, ignoring the woman, who was rudely inspecting us.

I knocked and waited. Behind me, the old woman said, "He ain't home."

My heart lurched, because I was really tired and hungry by that time, and I wanted to get inside right away. I reached up above the door, feeling for a key. Dad always used to leave a key over the door, though Mom said that was where everybody would look for one and it wasn't safe. In Marysville, though, nobody ever found it or used it.

Nothing. No key.

"Who're you?" the woman asked.

I almost told her it was none of her business, but for once I *did* think ahead. If Dad wasn't home, and we didn't have a key to his apartment, where were we going to go? What were we going to do? My stomach growled, and I knew we needed something to eat before long; it might pay to be civil to Dad's neighbors.

The old woman lived right across the hall. It would be nice if she were friendly.

"We're Vickie and Joanie Rakosi. Our dad lives in 3B," I said. "We were expecting him to be here to let us in."

"He ain't here," she repeated. "Saw him go out more'n an hour ago. Phone's been ringing all day, every time I was in the hall I heard it."

My nerves jerked. Gram, calling to see if we'd come here?

"Did you talk to him? Do you know where he went?"

She shook her head. "Didn't talk to him. Saw him from the window. I don't get out much, so I watch what's going on from the windows." It wasn't until then that I noticed she was leaning on a cane.

"If he knows you're coming, he'll probably be back pretty soon," she offered.

I swallowed. "He . . . doesn't know. I don't even know where he works, or if he works nights or what."

"Not nights," the old lady said. All of a sudden

she made Joanie and me jump because she balanced herself by touching the door frame with one hand and began to pound on the bare floor with her cane. That made the unseen dog bark again, and she paused long enough to say, "Shut up, George," before she pounded some more. Then she waited for a few seconds before she pounded again. She smiled at me, and I saw she was missing some of her teeth.

"The manager lives below me. Harold. He has a master key. He can let you in." She pounded again, more vigorously, and this time she bent over close to the floor, cautiously so as not to fall, and yelled, "Harold! Get up here! We got an emergency!"

We stood there, awkwardly, and a medium-sized dog appeared beside the woman. He was one of the ugliest dogs I ever saw, a bulldog. He stared at us with bulging eyes, then barked again, until the woman spoke sharply and thumped him with the cane.

A few minutes later we heard the elevator start down, and shortly after that Harold showed up, scowling. He was old, too, and crotchety when George barked at him. I wondered if the dog always heard the phrase, "Shut up, George," as often as he seemed to that night.

George stopped barking that time, too, but then he growled at the old man. Harold sort of growled back.

"One of these days," he told the woman sourly, "you're going to get to pounding with that thing and have a heart attack."

"Don't you hope! I know you want this apartment for your nephew. Don't know why. Shiftless as he is, he probably won't pay the rent after the first month and then you'll be stuck with it yourself. 'Course it would make your day to call the meat wagon for me, wouldn't it?"

Joanie looked as if she expected them to do physical combat any minute, and I wasn't sure, either.

"Might at that," the old man grunted. "What're you bellering about this time?"

"These here kids belong to the tenant in 3B. He ain't here to let 'em in."

He glared at her, and then at us. "So whose fault is that?" he demanded, but he was already searching through the keys he had clipped to his belt.

"Well, it sure ain't mine, but unless you want 'em camped in the hall all night, you better let 'em in," the old woman said.

"How do I know they're really his kids?" he grumbled, sticking a key into the lock of 3B.

"Oh, sure," the old woman said sarcastically. "You can tell by looking at 'em that they're spies or something. You want I should search 'em for weapons? Explosives? Drugs? Maybe they're his suppliers."

He twisted the knob and threw open the door of 3B, rolling his eyes. "Magda Kubelik, you're an old fool," he said.

To my surprise, she threw back her head and laughed. "So're you," she retorted, and withdrew into her own apartment, chortling. She almost closed the door on George, who was still glaring at us.

We stood there feeling confused and uncomfortable after she left, and Harold gestured at the door he'd opened for us. "There it is. Walk in. What're you waiting for?"

By this time I was beginning to get the idea that neither he nor the old woman was as hostile as I'd first thought.

"Thank you," I said with dignity, and hauled our suitcases into Dad's apartment.

Joanie looked relieved after I'd turned on the light. We were in a long, narrow living room. "I was afraid this was going to be a crummy place. I don't think I like old apartment houses. They're kind of scary."

"Just different from home," I told her. "Dad wouldn't live in a crummy place, not after what he was used to. Not if he had any money at all, and he's working now. Is there more than one bedroom?"

There was. It was plain which one was Dad's—his stuff was in the closet, and there was a small heap of change on the dresser, just like there always had been at home. Sometimes he'd give it to us if we got him in the right mood.

Joanie sniffed at the other bedroom. "One bed. Does that mean I have to sleep with you?"

"You can sleep on the floor if you want," I offered.

"I hate sleeping with you. You kick."

"Only when you take up three-quarters of the space."

"You don't cut your toenails. They scrape."

"So sleep on the floor," I said irritably. "Knock it off, Joanie. I told you not to come, so it's your own fault. What did you expect, Dad lived in the Taj Mahal or something?"

She scowled at me suspiciously. "What's that? That big fancy palace in India?"

"I think it's a mausoleum, not a palace," I said,

and then, before she could ask, I added, "It's a sort of tomb, where they store bodies."

"Why would I think Dad would live in a place like that?" she demanded.

"Oh, for pete's sake, Joanie! I just meant he wouldn't live in a luxury hotel; either adjust to the way it is or go home."

"I can't go home," she reminded me. "We only had one-way tickets and we haven't got enough money. I'm starved. I hope Dad's got something decent to eat."

"Well, let's haul our stuff into the bedroom we're going to be *sharing,* and then we'll find out," I said.

We went back through the living room. It looked as if he'd furnished it from a thrift store. There was a recliner chair in one corner, and a green couch and a desk, and a bookcase beside the chair. Dad always had books around him.

My throat tightened when I remembered how he'd asked Mom if she would mind if he took a particular book with him, and how she'd told him to take anything he wanted. They hadn't sounded like a man and a woman who hated each other, who were getting ready to get a divorce. In fact they'd been abnormally polite. That's what Gram said after Dad was gone.

"It's abnormal, Rosalie, to speak to each other as if you're still good friends," she said.

And Mom had not looked at her but responded in a quiet voice. "Steve and I are not enemies, Mother."

Not enemies. Could that mean they might someday be more than friends again?

We were disappointed in what was in the refrigerator—it didn't look as if Dad ever cooked much—but we found canned soup in the cupboard, and crackers. And there was chocolate ripple ice cream—Dad's favorite, and mine, too—in the freezer compartment.

We felt better after we'd had something to eat. Joanie was beginning to droop, so she took a shower and got ready to go to bed without even an argument. "I wish Daddy would come home before I go to sleep, though," she said when I turned down the bed for her.

"Me, too. But he'll probably be here in the morning." I giggled. "I guess he'll be surprised when he sees us."

Joanie looked younger than nine in her thin cotton pajamas with the tiny flowers all over them. "You going to listen to my prayers, Vic?"

"Sure," I agreed, and sat on the edge of the bed while she knelt beside it.

I really didn't listen to what she said, the way Mom and Gram did. I was thinking about Dad coming home and being surprised, and hoping he'd be glad we were there.

Somewhere not too far off I heard a cat crying. It was a lonely sound. I felt kind of lonely, too, being in a strange place and Dad not there.

When I turned out the light and wandered back into the living room, I flicked on the TV, but he didn't have cable, and there wasn't anything I wanted to watch on the regular channels. I turned it off and sat in the big chair, not yet ready to go to bed myself.

The cat was still crying.

After a few minutes I began to wonder if it was *inside* the apartment. I wasn't used to living in a building with other people in it who weren't members of the family, and it felt peculiar to hear someone else's music off in the distance, and a woman's angry voice, and a door slamming. It was strange and unfamiliar.

I felt suddenly homesick.

Now that is stupid, Victoria, I told myself. There's no one home except Gram, and you certainly aren't missing *her*.

The cat went on crying. Piteously.

A man yelled back profanities at the woman who had been shouting. There was a crash, and I pictured something heavy being thrown against a wall.

Jeez. How did anybody sleep in this place? Was it even safe here?

I wished Dad would come home. Where was he? What was he doing? Accountants usually work days, and besides, the old woman—what was her name? Magda Kubelick—had confirmed that he didn't work nights. Obviously she watched him coming and going, so she knew when he did it.

If he'd been at home in Marysville, I might have called one of his friends to see if they were together. Jack Scovil or Lon Whitcomb, he used to go bowling with them, or to a ball game. Or sometimes they sat around watching some sporting event on TV and eating junk food.

I didn't even know if he'd made any friends here in San Sebastian. It made me feel bad to think he might be really lonely, without any friends, in a strange town.

Gradually I realized I was smelling something familiar, but something I didn't expect to smell here.

Tobacco. Pipe tobacco. Grandpa Rakosi smoked a pipe, but Dad didn't. He always said he could think of plenty of more fun ways to die than smoking himself to death.

I got up and started looking around. And there it was, on top of the bookcase.

A pipe, a really stinky one.

Was Dad so lonely and depressed without us that he'd started smoking, even though he'd always said he was glad he'd never started and it would be stupid to begin now knowing how hazardous it could be?

I leaned over and smelled the pipe. It'd certainly been used recently.

I never thought Dad would give in and do something he'd always said was stupid. Not even if he was horribly lonely.

And then I saw something else.

There was a picture on the floor, one of those little snapshots you get in a booth at a dime store, that you snap yourself. It was a picture of a woman and a little girl.

They were both dark haired, laughing.

Was Dad seeing a woman? Was he with a woman now, someone other than Mom? A woman who had a little girl? Did Dad like another child, maybe better than he liked Joanie and me?

For a minute I felt dizzy and sick.

I didn't want to believe it. I didn't want to think about Dad meeting a woman with a kid, a woman I didn't know and didn't want to know.

I was suddenly scared, scared to know the truth. All this time since he'd left home, I'd kept hoping and believing that he and Mom would eventually get back together. I even made up stories about things that could happen to get Gram out of the picture so they'd have some privacy to work things out. My parents had almost never fought, at least that I knew of, though Dad and Gram had often exchanged angry words.

I wanted to cry.

I *did* cry, a little, when I went into the bedroom to get my pajamas. I was suddenly exhausted, and I didn't want to sit up any longer waiting for Dad. What would I do if he brought another woman home with him?

Joanie was sprawled sideways across the bed. I didn't see how such a small girl could take up so much of the total space. We'd had to sleep together when we visited Grandpa and Grandma Rakosi the time he gave me the hundred-dollar bill, and she'd done the same thing then. How could I have forgotten what it was like to sleep with her? Why hadn't I made her stay home where she belonged? Yet a part of me was kind of glad I wasn't here alone.

While I was getting my stuff out of the suitcase, Joanie flopped around into a different position, but she was still taking her half of the bed out of the middle. I paused long enough to drag her over onto her own side, and then I went and took a shower. I let the water run right in my face, hoping it would wipe away any traces of tears.

I was just getting out of the shower when the phone rang.

My heart started to hammer. It wouldn't be Dad, calling his own empty apartment, because he didn't know *we* were here.

It rang and rang and rang while I stood there, dripping. Gram, I thought. Would she send the cops to check if nobody answered?

It wouldn't be Mom, I thought. At least I didn't think so. Gram and Mom didn't talk to each other on the phone much when Mom was traveling, though Mom always left a number where she could be reached. This time, though, I thought she was going to be flying a lot from one place to another. And I wasn't sure Gram would want to call her and admit why we'd run away. She'd probably try to find us first, so Mom wouldn't have to interrupt her business trip and come home. Her boss would be really upset if she did that.

The ringing finally stopped, and I dried off and put on my pj's.

When I went back into the bedroom, Joanie was once more hogging the whole bed.

The heck with it, I decided, and took one pillow—she wasn't using either of them—and found a sheet. I went back to the couch in the living room.

I wasn't going to cry and get my nose all plugged up so I'd feel even more rotten than I already did. I threw the pillow down and myself after it and reached up to turn out the light. If Dad came home, with or without some female, he'd just have to find me there.

The room wasn't completely dark. The windows didn't have any shades, just curtains that sort of filtered the glow of the streetlights, and it was stuffy and too warm.

After a minute of trying to get comfortable, I got up and opened the windows, hoping there'd be a little breeze if the kitchen window was open, too.

I didn't think I'd be able to sleep, but the trip down here had been tiring. I was dozing off when something suddenly brought me wide awake.

What had I heard?

It could have been just another tenant in another apartment, but my heart was pounding with alarm.

And then the sound came again.

I peered through the dimness at the nearest of the windows, the one that looked out on the alley beside the building, and felt the hair rising on the back of my scalp.

A dark figure was silhouetted outside, and as I held my breath it parted the curtains and slid through the opening only a few yards from where I lay.

4

For a few seconds I felt frozen, and then anger surged through me and I proved Gram was right: I didn't always stop to think.

I reached out and turned on the light.

I blinked against the brightness. The intruder was blinking, too.

It was the boy from the front steps, without his harmonica, holding a big yellow striped cat with white on his front and paws. The cat made a plaintive sound and leaped out of the boy's arms, racing toward the kitchen.

I sat up and turned my back to the light. "Do you always go around breaking and entering late at night?" I asked, my fear fading.

"It wasn't breaking and entering. The window was wide open." He didn't sound apologetic. "You must have just opened it, or that fool cat would have come in by himself a couple of hours ago."

"I did just open it. Why would the cat have come in here?"

He looked at me as if I were retarded. "It lives here. Who're you?"

"Victoria Rakosi. Who're you?" I countered. From the next room, the cat's complaints reached a higher pitch.

He raised his voice to make it heard. "I'm Jake Ohanian. I live in the apartment above this one, and I was sick of listening to that darned cat. My dad has to get up early to go to work, and he said if the cat didn't stop yowling so he could get some sleep he was going to shoot it. So I brought it down the fire escape and was going to bring it inside and find it something to eat. We don't have any cat food, and we're out of tuna fish. It turned down baked beans and Jell-O salad."

"Are you sure it belongs here?" I demanded. "Dad never said anything about getting a cat." I frowned a little. "He'd never let us have one." Though come to think of it, it was Mom who had turned us down. Right about then I remembered that I was in pajamas, but they weren't the transparent kind so I decided it didn't make much difference.

"Belongs to the guy who lives here," Jake Ohanian stated. "He's only had it for a few days, I think. I heard him calling it in night before last. That bugged my old man, too. When he's bugged, he tends to yell at *me*. It's only been tonight that it was caterwauling around bothering the rest of the tenants. For pete's sake, feed it so it'll shut up."

"I don't know if there's anything to feed it," I said, getting up and heading for the kitchen. "When we were looking for groceries I didn't see any cat food."

He followed me and we finally located three cans

under the sink. Then I had to find a can opener, while the cat kept winding around my ankles and trying to trip me, crying all the way. I dumped half the contents of the can onto a saucer, and bent to read the tag on his collar.

"His name's Clancy. Irish, just like you."

"I'm not Irish. Ohanian is Armenian. If you hadn't been too stuck up to speak to me when you came in, I would have known you were here and I'd have just knocked on the door instead of coming through the window."

"I wasn't stuck up. I was just taught not to speak to strangers. Do you know my dad?"

"I've seen him a few times. He just nods or says hi. I read his name on the mailbox."

"Do you know where he works? What kind of hours?"

Jake shrugged, leaning against the door frame with his thumbs hooked in the pockets of the worn-out jeans. "I've seen him leaving about a quarter to eight in the morning. Haven't noticed what time he comes home. He must work somewhere close by. He walks, doesn't take a bus."

"I'm surprised he got a cat," I said, watching Clancy gobble the food as if he were starved. "I never thought he really liked cats."

"Maybe he picked up a stray. We aren't supposed to have dogs here, though Magda has that nasty little bulldog. She and the super are bosom buddies, so he lets her keep it, even though the rules say only cats."

"Magda's the lady across the hall? She's friends with the manager?" I asked, incredulous. "They insulted each other all over the place."

43

He was kind of cute when he laughed. He had nice teeth. "Yeah. You'd think they were mortal enemies. Magda's almost eighty, and Harold is seventy-six. My dad says trying to put one over on each other is all that keeps them going. Well, you got your cat back, and he's going to shut up so we can sleep, so I better go on back upstairs."

He turned around and headed for the window, and I followed him. "Does this mean it's not safe to leave this window open? Can everybody else come in the same way you did?"

He shook his head. "They could only come down from the fourth floor or up from 2B. No way to get up from the alley. If you keep the window up halfway, old Clancy can get in and out when he likes, and he won't yowl around our windows, okay?"

"Okay," I agreed. Then I couldn't help asking, "Do you see anyone else come here to visit my dad? Or come in with him?"

"Not that I noticed. He's only been here a few weeks, you know, and nobody's really gotten acquainted with him, I think. He's been alone every time I've seen him. Of course, Magda's the one to ask. She sits and watches out the window most of the time. If your dad's had company, she'll know. She knows everybody's business, whether they tell her or not."

He drew the curtains aside and swung a leg over the windowsill. A moment later I heard his feet on the metal grating of the fire escape.

After I was sure he was out of sight, I leaned out and inspected the stairs. He was right, nobody could come up from the alley unless someone from up here made the ladder drop to the ground level.

I guessed it was safe to go back to sleep. I had no sooner turned out the light than I felt the cat's feet land on my middle. It was startling, but sort of comforting, too, when Clancy curled up between me and the back of the couch. I stroked his head and went to sleep listening to his contented purring.

I didn't think I was nervous about some guy climbing in the window, or being in a strange town with nobody but Joanie. It was probably because the apartment was hot, and that fool cat was sleeping up against me, that made me dream.

I mean, I often dream, but the dreams don't usually scare me. And I'd never had a stranger come through a window into the room where I was sleeping before.

In the dream I heard the scrape of a key, and then another small sound when the lock clicked open. I even thought a light came on, though it wasn't very bright. I was so sleepy I didn't want to wake up, and I squeezed my eyes shut in protest, the way you do sometimes when you're dreaming something you don't want to dream. Mom said you can change the course of what's happening in a nightmare if you really try, and make the monsters go away.

There weren't any monsters in this one, actually. Just a shadowy figure looming over me, looking down at me. I squeezed my eyelids harder, and sure enough, he went away. I heard the latch click again when he left, and then it was dark again except for the filtered glow from the streetlight, through the curtains. I told myself I refused to have any more stupid bad dreams, and sure enough, Mom's method worked. I sank back into a deep sleep.

I woke up around dawn when I got chilly. I closed the window and pulled a sheet up over me. I vaguely remembered that tall figure from the dream, and for a minute I thought maybe Dad had come home but hadn't wanted to wake me up in the middle of the night.

I checked as soon as I got up, but his bed was empty, and there was no sign he'd been there. Disappointed, I decided it must have been a wishful-thinking kind of dream. Clancy was making hunger noises, so I gave him the cat food that was left over from last night.

I didn't know quite what to do about Dad not being there.

Joanie and I ate cornflakes and toast in the little kitchen while Clancy had the rest of the can of cat food. There were only two left.

"I don't really like cornflakes," Joanie said. "I wish we had some French toast. Or waffles."

I ground my teeth. "Stop griping. When Dad comes he'll get us something else, but until then, we're stuck with what's here, okay?"

"What if he doesn't come today?" she wanted to know.

I had just carried our dishes to the sink, and I threw open the cupboard doors just above it. "Then we eat macaroni and cheese or canned hash or peas."

"Yuck! Vickie, why didn't Dad come home last night?"

"How do I know?" I asked, though remembering

that picture I'd left on top of the bookcase gave me some uneasy suspicions. "But he probably went directly to work this morning from wherever he was. So maybe we better try to reach him there."

"Where does he work?" Joanie wanted to know.

"Good question. We'll have to do some detective work and find out," I said confidently. "There's probably something in the desk that will tell us."

There wasn't nearly as much as I'd hoped.

We found Mom's last letter to him, and without Gram around to stop me I went ahead and read it.

It wasn't as personal as I'd hoped, but it wasn't hostile, either. She told him about the marks we'd had at school, and that Joanie had fallen while skating and skinned her knees pretty badly, and that I'd had the lead in the school play. "I think," Mom had written, "that Vickie has a lot of you in her. Cornball, you know? It was a funny part, and everybody laughed in all the right places, and she remembered all her lines."

She'd signed it, not "with love," but "as ever, Rosalie."

As ever. Didn't that mean she felt the same way she used to about him? But she used to sign the notes she posted on the refrigerator, "Love, Rosie."

I sighed and put the letter back in the envelope.

In the desk I also found a receipt for the rent, an unpaid telephone bill, a notepad with nothing written on it, and a pay stub with deductions listed, from someplace called MCT, Incorporated, Local number 703.

MCT. That wasn't much to go on, and I couldn't find an MCT, Inc., in the phone book. "Hmm. Local number 703. Sounds like it might be a union," I mused. "Let's try the yellow pages for unions."

There was nothing there, but I finally thought to look under Labor Unions, and there was a listing for the Manufacturers Consolidated Trust, on East Delong Street, wherever that was.

"Did you find it?" Joanie asked, and I nodded. "Maybe. I'll call and see."

I dialed the number and a man's voice answered. "Local 703. Bryant speaking."

"Um," I said, because he sounded a lot more businesslike than friendly. "Do you have a Steve Rakosi working for you?"

I heard another phone ringing, and it sounded as if he'd picked it up, but then he spoke to me again. "Who's calling him?"

"I'm his daughter," I said, elated that I'd found him so easily.

Only I hadn't.

"Sorry, he's not working today," the man called Bryant said brusquely. "He called in sick."

My heart dropped. Sick? If he was sick, where was he? "Uh, do you expect him to be off for long?"

"I couldn't tell you," he said, and when another phone rang again, he hung up on me.

I stared at the telephone in frustration. "Dad's not working today, and the guy couldn't—or wouldn't—tell me when he'd be back."

"Why isn't he there, if that's where he works?"

"The guy said he called in sick," I said. "Dad never gets sick. Even that time when he mangled his finger in the lawn mower he got stitches in it and went to work."

Joanie scrunched up her face. "Maybe he lied. Maybe he's not really sick."

"Lied? Dad?" I demanded. But maybe he had. I mean on TV people lie about not being able to go to work because they're sick, when they really just want time off to do something else. Only what else would he be doing that would mean giving up a day's pay when he'd already been off work so long he *must* need the money? He'd really hoped that first job he'd taken in California would be a permanent one, but it had ended after only a few months. I was pretty sure he'd been flat broke when he got this one.

"Well," I said after a minute, "we can either sit here and wait until he shows up, or we can do some detective work and see if we can find him." It was unsettling to have Dad missing when I'd been so sure he'd be here. "I'm not much for waiting, so let's see what else we can do."

The trouble was he hadn't left any clues that I could find as to where he might be. Except, maybe, that picture on top of the bookcase. Why was there a picture in my dad's apartment of a woman and a little girl I'd never seen?

The idea that he might have found someone other than Mom was pretty upsetting. I didn't want him to be seeing someone else.

I checked his closet, and then the bathroom medicine cabinet, but I didn't find anything to suggest that a woman ever came there. The kitchen didn't look like a woman worked in it, either. The stove had greasy splatters nobody had wiped up, and all the food was easy-to-fix, stick-in-the-microwave kind of stuff. There weren't even any of the staples most women would have in their kitchens: no flour, sugar, spices, vinegar, that kind of thing. In fact, it wasn't the kind of kitchen that made me think *anybody* spent any time in it. It was sad that Dad had to live here by himself. It gave me hope that maybe he'd let Joanie and me stay. It didn't seem like he'd have stopped loving *us* even if he *had* made friends with someone else.

I didn't know whether to worry about him being sick or to believe Joanie was right, that he'd lied about it to get time off. I didn't remember him ever doing anything like that before, though. It hurt to think he might have lied.

When I walked back past the desk, I stared at the notepad, then picked it up. When it was tilted so the light struck it just right, I could see the imprint of the last thing that had been written. I penciled in the outlines so I could read it—a telephone number. On impulse, I dialed it, and got a busy signal.

Joanie was leaning on the end of the desk, waiting expectantly. At her feet the cat, Clancy, meowed and rubbed against her, and Joanie picked him up. She'd been delighted to find a cat in residence. We'd never been allowed to have one at home, though she'd begged and begged. It sure didn't seem fair that Dad had one now, when he hadn't taken our side against Mom when we asked for a kitten.

Clancy sprang out of her arms and stalked to the window, which was now closed. He cried plaintively and looked back at us.

"I think he wants out," Joanie said.

"Brilliant deduction," I told her, and she stuck her tongue out at me.

I went over to open the window for him, since apparently he couldn't escape the building unless he leaped all the way to the street level. He was through the opening in a flash, and immediately scampered up the stairs to the upper floor.

"He must have cut himself," Joanie said as I was turning away from the window. "See, he made a bloody footprint in the windowsill."

I stopped, bent closer to see the smudge on the cream-colored paint, and then drew in a deep breath.

It wasn't a cat's paw-print, though I was pretty sure it was blood all right.

It was the print of a man's thumb. And when my gaze dropped downward, I saw three big splotches of the dark reddish stain in the green rug.

Someone had gone through that window, and he'd either been bleeding himself or had touched someone else's blood just before he went over the sill.

5

I wondered if I ought to look through the apartment for a body. I mean, what if the guy killed somebody and then escaped through the window?

The most likely person to have been killed in my dad's apartment was my dad.

"Whose blood is it?" Joanie asked while I struggled with a moment of panic.

"I don't know. Maybe we better look around and see if there's any more of it," I said. "I wonder if it was there last night when that Ohanian kid brought the cat back?"

I'd told Joanie about him when she found Clancy with me that morning and pounced on him with delight.

"Maybe the boy left it," Joanie suggested.

"I don't think so. It's a really big man's thumbprint." I pulled the curtain aside to see if I'd have noticed it when I put Clancy back out on the fire escape. Maybe not, I concluded. The curtains covered that part of the sill when I pulled them apart to make room for him to get out. A man would have had to get all the open space possible, so if the curtains were wide open he could easily have left the print. The barely visible spots on the carpet were covered, too, as long as the curtain hung in place.

"There's more blood on the floor," Joanie said, squatting to examine it more closely. "Look, Vickie, isn't this the same kind of stain over here?"

I knelt beside her. "It sure looks like it. Let's check around and see if there's any more."

There was. Near one side of the bookcase we found a patch of the carpet that not only was a little darker than the rest, it was even still damp.

I stared at it, feeling queasy.

"Is it more blood?" Joanie asked in a hushed voice.

I swallowed. "I don't know. Get me a paper towel."

She brought one from the kitchen, and gingerly I rubbed it over the damp spot, and examined the towel.

"It's not blood," Joanie said in relief. "It's maybe strawberry pop or something like that, pale pink."

I ran my tongue over my lips. "I don't think so. I think it . . . it was blood, and somebody scrubbed most of it up."

Then I saw her face and was sorry I'd spoken my thoughts. She rocked back on her heels and stared at me in consternation. That was another word she'd have known, because Gram accused me of enjoying Mom's consternation when I did something wild, which was ridiculous. Whenever I did whatever I did, I wasn't thinking about what anyone would think. I was only thinking about what would be fun, or at least interesting, to *me.*

But Mom would probably be feeling about the same as I was over this, and it sure wasn't my fault this time.

Joanie's lips formed the words very softly. "Whose blood?"

I didn't answer that. "Let's look around and see if there are any more stains or damp spots."

It was kind of grisly, crawling around the living room rubbing my hands over the rug, looking for more blood spots.

The trouble was, we found two more. When I rubbed them with the damp paper towel, that faint pink showed up again.

"It's not Dad's, is it? Somebody couldn't have killed him, could they?" Joanie asked, almost in a whimper.

"He called in sick, remember? So he couldn't have been dead," I reminded her.

"Maybe it wasn't him that called in and said that," Joanie whispered, and I began to be sorry I'd let her stay up late with me to watch those scary movies. "Maybe somebody else called and said they were him."

I stood up, and wasn't surprised to find that my legs were shaking. "I don't think it's Dad's," I said, for no logical reason I could think of. After all, it *was* his apartment. "But something strange happened here. I think we better find out what it was."

"How?" Joanie wanted to know.

"That Jake Ohanian said the old lady across the

hall sees everything that goes on. She knows about everybody else's business, whether they tell her or not."

Magda didn't know about this, though. Not that I told her about the blood, of course. I wasn't that stupid.

I wasn't sure she'd even let us in when we knocked, but she did. The dog barked, and she yelled, "Shut up, George!" and then opened the door.

"Oh, it's you two. Smelled my cookies baking, eh?"

"No," I said. "Could we talk to you for a few minutes, though?"

"Why not? Come on in. Get out of the way, George."

Her apartment looked pretty much like Dad's except everything was backward. She had a rocker instead of a recliner, as well as a flowered couch, where we were invited to sit. She brought a plate of the cookies—we could smell them as soon as she opened the door—and we each took one, just to be polite. I wasn't really hungry, or at least I didn't think so before I took a bite.

"Your dad glad to see you, was he?" Magda asked. I was relieved that as soon as we all sat down, the bulldog curled up on the throw rug by her feet, though he continued to inspect us with those bulging eyes.

I cleared my throat. "He hasn't come home yet," I said. "We thought maybe you'd seen something . . . or heard something. I mean—you *saw* him leave a while before we got here, right? And he was alone?"

Magda nodded. "I just happened to be standing

at that front window when he left. Never saw him with anyone else since he came here. Listen, didn't he know you kids were coming?"

"Uh," I said, trying to think fast, "well, he didn't know exactly *when*." I didn't want her to poke into that. "He seemed okay? Not . . . sick or . . . hurt?"

She shook her head and helped herself to a cookie. "Looked all right to me."

"And you're sure it was Dad? I mean, you look down from that window, right? Maybe it's hard to get a good look from up above."

"Oh, I saw him plain enough to know it was him. I mean, nobody else in the place has a black beard." Magda munched and dropped a piece of cookie for George. He swallowed it in one gulp and licked up the crumbs.

"Dad has a beard?" Joanie blurted.

I'd warned her to keep still and let me do the talking, but I was surprised, too. "We didn't know he'd grown a beard," I said. "He used to have one before, though. When he and Mom first married. She didn't like it, so he shaved it off." And now, I thought, it didn't matter what Mom thought, so he'd grown one again.

A thought occurred to me. "Did you see him when he was moving in?"

Magda shrugged. "What's to see when a bachelor moves? Carried in a couple suitcases, three or four cardboard boxes, a few pieces of furniture."

"He had his car? A blue Pontiac?"

She nodded. "That's right."

"Where do people who live here leave their cars?" Jake had said Dad walked to work, but if he'd left to go anywhere else he would probably have taken the car.

"They just park 'em on the street. Nobody's supposed to block the alley on that side of the building, the garbage trucks have to go through, but if you go all the way to the back there's a few spaces out behind. I think your dad parks out there."

I'd check that out as soon as we left here. "Did he have a cat?" I asked.

"A cat? No cat." At her feet, George lifted his large head and made whoofing sounds.

Magda grinned, showing the gaps in her teeth. "George likes cats, don't you, George?"

"Does he eat them?" Joanie asked, looking as if she already knew the gory answer.

"No, no, though he may chase strange ones. We had two cats when George was a pup, and they used to curl up together to sleep. No, your dad didn't bring any cat in that I ever saw. Why, is there one there now? Or are you missing one?"

"There's one there now. His collar says his name is Clancy. He . . . was crying and upset Mr. Ohanian, upstairs."

She made a snorting noise. "Everything upsets Krikor Ohanian. That man has the disposition of a wasp. Every time anybody slams a door he complains. Or drops a dish. Or turns the TV up loud enough to hear it." She rubbed George with one slippered foot. "Or barks. Eh, George?"

"Did you hear anything unusual yesterday?" I asked, trying to think like a detective. "Just before Dad went out, or right afterward?" There was always a chance, I thought desperately, that someone else had been in the apartment after he'd gone, that he didn't know anything about the bloodstains.

Her eyebrows went up. "Unusual? I don't know what'd be unusual around here. Mrs. Albertoni screaming at her kids. The Smith baby crying. Krikor yelling about something. Fire engines screeching up to fires. Old Becker turns up his TV so loud he drowns out almost everything else. That's mostly what I heard yesterday, early evening. His cops-and-robbers shows. Sirens screaming, gunshots. I wish he'd listen to some nice music once in a while."

"Gunshots?" I asked, my mouth suddenly dry. Could someone have been shot in Dad's apartment yesterday? It couldn't have been any longer ago than that or the carpet wouldn't still be damp where somebody'd cleaned it up.

She rocked and nodded. "Sometimes we even hear real ones, though this is a pretty quiet neighborhood most of the time. Had a fire down the block the other day. Couple of weeks ago some customers over at the Watering Hole took potshots at each other. They weren't sober enough to hit anything, but the cops came and hauled them both away." She dropped another half cookie to George. No wonder he was kind of fat.

I tried to word my question carefully, to sound as if it didn't really matter. "Did those gunshots sound different from the ones on Mr. Becker's TV? I mean, louder, or closer, or anything?"

"Louder? Not really. He's deafer than a kumquat."

She leaned over to pass the plate around again, and Joanie took a second cookie, but my stomach was in cramps, and I shook my head. "I've never heard any gunshots," I said. "I just wondered if the real ones sounded different."

"Not that I noticed. In fact, I thought it was the TV until I heard the ruckus out in the street. Everybody but me and George went out to gawk when the ambulance came."

What else could I ask to get any useful information? I sucked in a breath and tried to clear my head. "Have you noticed any strangers lately? Coming or going? You know, people who don't live here but came to visit or something?"

Magda stopped chewing. She stared at me more intently. "Strangers? Why are you asking about strangers?"

I tried to think of a logical reason. "Well, I just wondered if any of Dad's friends might have picked him up. If for some reason he stayed over with one of them last night instead of coming home."

Magda began to rock again, scratching behind George's ear with one foot. "Never saw him have any company at all, until you two showed up. That Ohanian kid might have seen 'em if anybody did. He was sitting down there on the front steps playing that same stupid song over and over again last night, right up to dark. I shut the window so I couldn't hear him so plain. Have another cookie."

This time I took one. I'd eat it later when I wasn't so tense. "Well, thank you," I said, getting up, and Joanie stood up, too.

"I hope your dad comes home tonight," Magda said. "He prob'ly will."

"We hope so, too," Joanie said. It was a miracle she'd been quiet that long. "We need him to buy some decent groceries."

"Running out, are you?" Magda frowned.

"Not yet," I said quickly. "She just doesn't like what's in the cupboard. And most likely he'll show up before long."

Only he didn't.

I'd never been any more scared in my whole life, and I almost wished I was still at home, even if Gram *was* the only one there.

There were bloodstains on the carpet, enough of them to convince me somebody had been seriously hurt. I prayed that nobody had died, and that Dad wasn't either a victim or a murderer; and I couldn't think what to do next.

6

Jake Ohanian got off the elevator as we were leaving Magda Kubelik's apartment. He waved and called out a greeting.

"Bearding the dragon and her monster already this morning?" he asked. He'd washed his hair and he looked much better.

Magda had come with us to the door and had not yet closed it, so she heard him. She stared at him, said, "All mouth, that boy," and closed the door on us.

Jake was grinning. "She expects me to say something friendly, the way Harold does," he explained. "Your old man show up?"

"No," I told him. "He didn't."

He stopped grinning. "You haven't heard from him or anything?"

Joanie had her eyes fixed on his face, and before I could guess what she meant to do and stop her, she said, "Somebody bled all over in dad's apartment."

He started to grin again, thinking it was a joke, but when he met my gaze he decided she meant it.

"Bled?" he repeated. "You kidding?"

"Real blood," Joanie said soberly.

"Well, we didn't have it analyzed," I said. I hadn't intended to confide in him, but now that she'd let the cat out of the bag, it was a relief. "But we're pretty sure it's blood. There's a bloody thumbprint on the windowsill. You weren't bleeding when you went through the window, were you?"

Maybe a part of me was hoping he *had* been, and that there was a logical and nonfrightening explanation for what was going on, because when he shook his head I felt my stomach going into a knot again.

"Not that I noticed," Jake said. Interest brightened his face. "Let's see it."

Well, why not?

I hadn't locked the door when we left Dad's apartment to cross the hall, because we didn't have a key to get back in. I led the way, and then Joanie ran ahead and pulled aside the curtain to show him the thumbprint.

Jake stared at it. "Umm. A big man, I'd say."

"Unless he climbed up to your place, he must have gone down the fire escape." I wanted him to come up with a reasonable scenario of what had probably happened, one that wouldn't mean Dad was mixed up in something horrible.

"There's more on the floor," Joanie offered.

Jake squatted down and looked at the stains that had been hidden by the curtain, then felt the damp spot where the carpet had been scrubbed. "Must have been in a hurry when they wiped up," he observed.

"How do you figure that?" I asked sharply.

"If they'd had time, they'd have done a better job. Moved the curtain and made sure there was none under there, for instance. Is this the only place?"

We showed him the other spots. "It's still not quite dry, so it couldn't have been done earlier than yesterday, I figure. Say just before we came." I waited for his reaction to that.

He sounded thoughtful. "Could be. If they really soaked the rug, trying to get the blood out, it might possibly have been a day earlier. I spilled a pitcher of grape Kool-Aid once and it took several days to dry out, even after I soaked up as much as I could with towels. Never did get the purple out. We wound up putting a chair over the stain." He stood up. "Was it all here, in the living room?"

For some reason I felt guilty. "I don't know. We didn't look anywhere else. We didn't notice anything more."

"Let's check," Jake said, and moved toward the hall with the bathroom and bedrooms opening from it.

A part of me resented the assured way he took over, and at the same time it seemed like maybe another viewpoint might be worthwhile. I hadn't figured out that the cleanup job had been hurried, though it seemed right when he pointed it out.

When he jerked open the closet door in the hall I held my breath, but there were no bodies in the coat closet. No bloodstains. In fact it was empty except for an old vacuum cleaner.

Dad's things were in one bedroom. The closet looked almost empty compared to the way it had been at home, when his stuff and Mom's both hung in the same place and her clothes crowded his off to one end.

I hadn't hung up anything we'd brought with us yet, and I was surprised to find a few things in the closet in what I thought of as *our* bedroom: a pair of gray slacks, a blue-and-white striped shirt with a blue tie draped around the hanger, and a pair of running shoes.

I stared at them as Joanie asked, "How come Dad put some of his stuff in here when his own closet's mostly empty?"

"I'm not sure it's his," I said slowly. "Do these look like any clothes you remember Dad having?"

"No, but he's been gone for quite a while. Maybe he got some new things."

"I don't think so," I said slowly.

"Why not?" Jake asked at once.

"Because I doubt if he had any money to spend on clothes. I mean, he was out of work for a while, and I'm pretty sure he ran up some bills. And he hasn't been working very long at this MCT place. I doubt if he could afford to buy clothes."

"That where he works? At the union office?" Jake was feeling in the pockets of the slacks. "No wonder he walked to work. That's only three blocks over." He pulled his hand out of the pants. "Book of matches. From"—he turned it to read the lettering on the cover—"the Seven Palms. That's a night spot out on Gardena Avenue. South end of town. Go-go dancers and maybe illegal gambling, from what I've heard."

"Dad wouldn't go to a place like that!" Joanie said indignantly.

I wouldn't have thought so, either, but after what we'd discovered in the past twenty-four hours I was no longer sure of anything.

Jake dropped the matches onto the top of the dresser. "Maybe this stuff doesn't belong to your dad. Maybe it's in here because he had a guest who used this room. Check the shoe sizes." He bent to look inside the running shoes. "Size twelve double A."

We all crossed the hallway to Dad's room. Jake read the label out of the nearest pair of shoes. "Twelve and a half double E."

Puzzled, Joanie looked from Jake to me. "What's that mean? They're both Daddy's shoes?"

"Not likely," Jake said.

At the same time I reasoned aloud, "Dad couldn't get his feet into a shoe as narrow as a double A."

"So he had company, and the guy left a few of his things here," Jake said. "Maybe that's where your dad is now, visiting *him*. I didn't see any sign of any more blood in here. Whatever it was that happened, it took place in the living room. And somebody went out the window."

"Magda says Mr. Becker watches cop shows," I said. "With sirens and gunshots. So if somebody shot a gun here everybody who heard it might think it was his TV."

65

"Or it had a silencer," said Joanie. "Then nobody'd hear it at all, would they?" I was definitely going to have to pay more attention to the kind of TV programs she watched.

Jake led the way back out into the living room while we all thought about it. The whole thing was making me very nervous.

Jake crossed to the window and threw it wide open, allowing Clancy back inside. I spoke to Jake's back.

"Were you sitting on the front steps for a long time last night? Before we came, I mean?"

"Yeah, most of the time. It was so hot upstairs I stayed out where it was cooler. It's been like this for a couple of weeks. The whole neighborhood moves out onto the steps."

"You said you didn't see my dad come in or out."

He paused, holding the curtains aside as he swung a leg over the windowsill. "Nope."

"Nor any stranger, either?"

"Nope. Nobody but the people who live here. Listen."

A siren screamed toward us, rising and falling. Jake twisted around so he could watch toward the street. "Another fire, or maybe that's an aid car. No, it's an ambulance. Not coming here, anyway."

My mind caught on a few of his words. "*Another* fire? Did you just have one?"

"Not here in the apartment house. There was one night before last in the next block. Some old geezer fell asleep with a cigarette and set his chair on fire. We all went trooping up there to watch them put it out. They had to take the old man to the hospital for smoke inhalation, so nobody was sitting on the steps then. Rotten old George escaped from Magda's apartment while the rest of us were at the fire, and he nipped a couple of people before she caught him. Mr. Becker would have killed him if he'd had a gun, I guess, and he never did get to the fire, so fighting off George was the only excitement he saw. But last night I was out front from suppertime until after dark. No strangers."

Clancy, having checked out his dish, sprang up beside Jake and then on through onto the fire escape, vanishing upward. I hoped Mr. Ohanian was working and not home where the cat would bother him.

"What're you doing?" I asked Jake, forgetting the cat.

"Checking for blood out here. If he used it at night, when he was bleeding, he might not have noticed if he left any traces."

The curtains would have fallen back into place, but I held them apart and stuck my head through the opening after him as Jake squatted to examine the fire escape platform.

"Nothing here," he reported, and then began to descend toward the second floor. A moment later he made a little sound of triumph. "More blood here. I'm pretty sure it's blood. Get me a wet paper towel, will you?"

When I'd handed it down to him, he scrubbed at the rusty-looking spots, then held the towel up so I could see it.

"Blood," I said hollowly. "Somebody was still bleeding when he went down."

"Well, at least he was still alive, not dead."

"How do we know that?" I demanded.

"Well, he kept moving. He got down off the fire escape. Of course," Jake mused, "he could have been dead and somebody *dragged* him down."

I groaned. That scenario didn't appeal too much, either.

"We've got to figure out where Dad is," I said uneasily. "Make sure he's okay. Only I don't know where to look. The guy who answered the phone where he works said he was off sick today and they didn't know when he'd be back."

"Daddy never gets sick," Joanie said helpfully.

Jake slid back over the sill into the living room. "Did you call his friends?"

"We don't know who they are, or even if he had any here. He hasn't been here very long. I mean, he's been in California, but he was moving around, looking for a job. He had a few temporary ones, but I'm not sure where."

Jake prowled around the living room as if looking for clues. "Does he have an address book? Or, you know, a little notebook for phone numbers, that kind of stuff?"

"No, not that we found. I think he *had* one, but he carried it with him. Just a little one." I walked over to the desk and picked up the notepad. "He tore off the top sheet, but you can still read the numbers where he pressed hard enough to make an impression on the next sheet. He left this."

I handed the pad to him, and Jake studied the number I'd traced. "Whose number is it? Did you call them?"

"I got a busy signal. I didn't get a chance to try again." I hesitated. "And there's a picture on the bookcase, of a woman and a little girl. I don't know who they are." It hurt to say it, because I was afraid of what it might mean.

"Let's see it," Jake said, and I turned toward the bookcase to get it. The picture wasn't there.

I frowned at Joanie. "Did you take it and put it down somewhere else?"

"No. I never touched it."

"But it was right there," I insisted. "Last night."

"Who else has been in here since then?" Jake asked.

"Nobody. Joanie, are you sure you didn't move it?"

She was scowling, too. "I *told* you, Vic. I didn't touch it. Maybe Clancy knocked it off."

We looked. There was no picture behind the bookcase, or anywhere else.

"It *has* to still be here," Joanie said, frowning. "How could it go anywhere by itself?"

And then I remembered the dream.

I went very still, feeling shocked.

What if I hadn't dreamed it? What if there really had been a man standing over me? What if *he* had taken the picture?

Jake was watching my face. "What did you remember?"

My tongue snaked over suddenly dry lips, and I

swallowed. "I don't know if I . . . remember or . . . I *thought* it was a dream."

Now they both stared at me. "What?" Jake prompted.

"I slept there on the couch last night. Because Joanie hogs the bed so bad."

Joanie squealed a protest, but I kept on talking over her objections.

"I dreamed I heard a key in the lock, and somebody coming in. It was like I half woke up, but not all the way, and I saw someone standing over me, looking down at me."

Joanie forgot her indignation. "Who was it?"

"I don't know. A man. A *big* shadowy man."

"Dad?" Joanie asked.

"I don't know," I said slowly, closing my eyes to slits the way they'd been when I saw him. "His back was to the light, and I couldn't see his face, just . . . deep shadows."

"Did you leave the light on when you went to sleep?" Jake wanted to know. "You didn't have a light on when I brought the cat down, but if you were nervous after I left—"

"I wasn't the least bit nervous," I denied. "And no, I didn't leave a light on. Whatever this was from, it was a very dim light."

Jake glanced around, then walked to the door and flicked the switch beside it. A miniature bulb came on in the fixture in the tiny entryway.

"A dim light," he said unnecessarily. "You heard a key, you saw a dim light. Could have been this one. And it would have been behind anybody who stood by the couch and looked down at you."

A prickle of horror crept up my spine.

It was worse than it had been the time I jumped off the top of the Kavorkians' barn with the home-made parachute Hank had attached to me, and I realized it wasn't going to keep me from crashing into the chicken house and breaking my neck. Well, it had been my arm that fractured, not my neck, but I'd known before I hit that it was going to *hurt*.

This was scarier, much scarier.

"But Dad's the only one who'd have a key, isn't he?" Joanie asked, confused and beginning to be scared, too. "And *he* wouldn't have just . . . looked at Vickie, and gone away!"

"He could have picked up the picture," Jake pointed out, demonstrating how easily it could have been scooped off the top of the bookcase. "Your dad's a big guy. Do you think it was him?"

I had to swallow again. "I don't know. I don't *think* so. It didn't . . . *feel* like Dad. I didn't see his face," I concluded helplessly.

Jake scratched his head thoughtfully. "Curiouser and curiouser," he said.

Alice's Adventures in Wonderland is one of Joanie's favorite books, so she recognized the quote and didn't have to ask for an explanation. "What's going on?" she asked forcefully.

"I wish I knew," I said, chewing on my lower lip.

"Well," Jake said, suddenly grinning. "Looks like we've got a mystery to solve."

He was enjoying this situation. But I couldn't. It was *my* dad who was missing, with blood all over his apartment, and Joanie and I were stuck here by ourselves, and maybe somebody else had a key.

I felt the hairs rising on my scalp, and I tried to think what in the heck to do next.

This was the nightmare, and I was wide awake.

7

"Are we going to call the police?" Joanie asked.

"Why would we do that?" I demanded.

"Well, because of all the blood. Maybe somebody got killed."

"And what if . . . if Dad's the one who did it?" It made my chest ache to think about it. "Do we want to turn him in, without even knowing exactly what happened?"

"We can't turn him in. We don't know where he is," Joanie pointed out. "And what if he *didn't* do anything wrong? What if he's the one who's hurt? What if he's in terrible trouble and needs help?"

"Then we need to find him and help him," I said, almost under my breath. "Let's try calling that number again. You do it this time, Jake." I was almost afraid to find out whose number it was.

"Okay." Jake picked up the phone and dialed, then held the phone so I could hear, too.

I moved in close so our shoulders were touching. This time it didn't go unanswered.

"San Sebastian Memorial Hospital. May I help you?"

Hospital?

Why would Dad have written the phone number of the hospital on his notepad?

I tried to get my mind in gear, but Jake's worked faster.

"Do you have a Steve Rakosi as a patient?" he asked.

"One moment, please," the woman said.

We waited, me holding my breath, until she came back on the line. "No, I'm sorry, we have no one by that name," she said.

We couldn't think of anything else to ask. Jake thanked her and hung up. "Maybe he's got a friend in there. Maybe," he said, brightening, "whoever got hurt here. Maybe it was an accident to his friend, and he took him to the hospital, and that's where he's been instead of coming home."

It was possible, I supposed. "I like that idea better than that somebody was murdered," I admitted. "But we don't have any way to know his friend's name."

But already Jake was backing off. "I wonder how they got a wounded man out of here? I mean, nobody saw them go out the front door or the whole place would know about it. And if they'd called an ambulance, we'd all know. No, whoever was bleeding went out the window and down the fire escape."

"Why would he do that? Except to keep from being seen." I slumped onto a chair. "So where do we go from here?"

"Makes you wonder," Jake said thoughtfully. "It doesn't make any sense to take a wounded man down a fire escape unless they were involved in something illegal."

I straightened up. "Illegal! You've got to be crazy!"

Jake regarded me as if *I* were the one with the loose marbles. "Are you sure you know your dad? You don't think he'd bet with a bookie, you don't think he'd go to a nightclub where they have dancing girls, you don't think he'd stab or shoot anybody so they'd bleed all over the place. And he didn't have a beard when you last saw him, you told Magda. I don't think you know very much about him."

I was beginning to think the same thing, but I didn't like hearing it from Jake. "I know he's a good, decent, hardworking man who cares about his family. And he's honest. He wouldn't be mixed up in anything . . . crooked."

For a moment Jake's eyes challenged me. Then he picked up the pad and studied the number written there. "Why would he have the hospital number written down unless he knew somebody in there that he might want to talk to?"

"Maybe he called them when somebody got hurt," Joanie said, "and told them he was bringing his friend in, so they'd be ready when he got there. Or to ask their advice about first aid."

Jake shrugged. "Could be. So if he didn't take whoever got hurt to the hospital, he took him home, and stayed there with him."

I hit a fist on the edge of the desk. "And we have no way of knowing *where*!"

Joanie was staring at the notepad. "Did you trace the number the way it really looked, Vickie?"

I wished she'd shut up so I could think. "Yes, I followed the letters that were dented into the paper," I told her impatiently.

"Then why doesn't it look like Daddy's writing?"

I stared at her, then reached to pick up the notepad while Jake maneuvered around so he could inspect it, too, though of course he'd never seen Dad's writing.

I scowled. She was right. It had always been a joke at our house, how Dad could be so untidy about so many other things but that his writing—particularly his numbers—was so neat and legible.

These didn't look like his numbers. Especially the seven. This wasn't the way he'd have written a seven.

I had to admit it. "Somebody else must have written the hospital phone number. So where does that leave us?"

We didn't get around to answering that, even if we'd had an answer, because at that moment we heard a fearful racket out on the fire escape.

Joanie opened the window to see what was going on, and poor Clancy sprang into her arms, yowling and spitting. A second or two later, we saw why.

George was hot on his heels, barking ferociously. He'd have come right on through the open window if Jake hadn't been filling the space by that time.

"Get down, George! Knock it off," Jake ordered. He stuck his head out the window and glanced down, and when I joined him, I could see Magda on the next floor down.

"Come here, George," the old woman commanded, and the bulldog drew back, panting. "Sorry about that. I was sitting here visiting with Mrs. Albertoni when some cat showed up on the fire escape, and George went right out the window after it. Come down, George."

George's tongue was hanging out, and I wondered if he wasn't too old and too fat to deal with that much activity. He didn't make any move to go down the iron steps.

"Come down, George! You hear me, you dratted dog?"

"He may be scared of the open steps," Jake said after a moment, while George continued to sit there, whining. "He was excited enough about chasing Clancy so he didn't notice, coming up, but now he can see through to the ground. I'll bring him in through the window and take him over to your apartment," he offered.

I spoke over my shoulder to Joanie. "Take Clancy out of sight, and hang on to him."

George was pretty big and heavy for even Jake to manage, and he didn't like being picked up. Without a collar or a leash, though, he was impossible to drag. But Jake got him inside. Magda shouted orders up from the second-floor window.

"Just put him outside my door and tell him to stay. He'll wait until I get up there in a minute or two."

"Okay," Jake agreed, and half staggered across the living room to where I opened the door for him.

"Stay, George," Jake told the dog when he'd deposited him across the hallway. "You understand?"

George whined, eyes bulging, then barked.

"Shut up, George," I said from our doorway, and he looked at me, but didn't bark again.

"Jeez," Jake said, wiping slobber off his shirt as he came back into our apartment.

I forgot about George as I closed the door behind Jake. "I wonder if it would do any good to go over to the hospital and see if I can find my dad?"

He shrugged. "You can try. It's pretty big, though. It's the only one in the county, so they handle a lot of patients. You might have to walk around peeking into every room, if they'd let you."

"You don't think if I talked to the people in charge and described Dad—with a dark beard, I mean— that someone might have noticed if he's there?"

"Maybe. It's worth a try. You'd have to walk about three miles."

I thought about how hot it was out there, and twice times three miles is six. "Maybe I could try calling again. Ask for the person in charge and see if anyone's seen a man with a beard there with a patient. Especially if he stayed all night, someone might have noticed him."

So I called, and talked to a lady who said she was the assistant administrator. She didn't know anything about Dad but said she'd make inquiries, and she took my number.

"Maybe your little sister is right," Jake said. "About calling the police, if he doesn't turn up pretty soon."

I bit my lip. "But what if . . . he's in trouble, and calling the police would make it worse?"

"If he shot or stabbed somebody, would you cover for him?" Jake asked bluntly.

I hesitated. "I don't know. He . . . he always said to do what's right, and I can't believe he'd ever . . . do anything bad. Not really bad. Anyway, I'd have to know what happened before I could decide, I guess. On TV people get mixed up in bad things without meaning to, and maybe that's what's going on now."

Jake nodded. "Yeah, I can relate to that. I mean, my old man yells a lot, and he used to use his belt on me when I got out of line. But he's honest, too, and I don't think he'd ever deliberately break the law. Holy cow, what's that?"

"That" was obviously George. We both made a dash for the door.

We could hear the bulldog barking and snarling, but we couldn't see him. Magda had just stepped out of the elevator, and recognized her pet's voice.

"George! George!" she yelled, but she had to lean heavily on her cane, and she couldn't move very fast.

"Where is he?" I yelped as I followed Jake along the hallway toward Magda.

"On the stairs," Jake said over his shoulder, and then just before we all met at the top of them we heard bodies falling, somebody swearing, and George going absolutely crazy.

Magda stopped at the top of the stairs while Jake and I pounded down the first flight, turned the corner, and practically fell over Mr. Becker, who was sprawled on the steps, blocking our way.

George was farther below us, around the next bend in the stairway, still barking hysterically.

"George! George!" Magda sounded as frantic as

her dog was, and people were beginning to come out of their apartments and ask what was going on.

Mr. Becker, for once, had nothing unpleasant to say. He dragged himself into a sitting position, and Jake bounded past him, and I either had to stop or step on the old man's outstretched legs. I stopped.

He was dazed, and there was a scrape on his nose that was oozing a few bright red drops.

"Did George attack you?" I asked uncertainly. Below, I could still hear the dog, and Jake's raised voice trying to calm him down.

Mr. Becker didn't answer. He lifted one hand and looked at it, and that was pretty well scraped up, too.

"George! Is George all right?" Magda called from the third-floor level.

He sounded perfectly healthy to me. I turned my head to call out that Jake had gone after him, but before I got out more than a couple of words I heard my little sister.

"Clancy! No, Clancy, come back!" Her voice rose in a shriek.

I rounded the bend in the stairs in time to see Clancy scoot between Magda's legs, just as she took a shaky step downward.

There was nothing I could do except watch in horror as the old woman pitched forward and came tumbling toward me on the stairs.

Clancy spat and hissed, practically flying past me.

Magda stopped falling about halfway up from the

landing where I stood, and Joanie appeared at the top, her face white with shock.

She looked down at Magda and asked tremulously, "Is she dead, Vickie?"

8

It took about ten minutes to get everything under control. Magda wasn't dead, but she'd knocked herself senseless, and though Mr. Becker was conscious, he was stunned and shaken. At first he didn't respond when I spoke to him.

That fool bulldog continued to bark until Jake bellowed, "*Shut up, George!*" and he finally stopped. Jake appeared below me, carrying Clancy, who was trying to climb on his head to get away from George. Jake thrust the cat at me.

"Get him out of here," he said, then looked in dismay at Magda. "Good grief, what happened to *her?*"

"She started to come down the stairs and Clancy tripped her," I said, nearly crying. "She's knocked out. He went right between her feet."

Joanie was looking like a little ghost up above me, and I reached up to give her the cat, passing him over Magda's limp body. I could see she was still breathing, but she wasn't moving.

"Close Clancy in the apartment," I told Joanie. "I think we'd better call an ambulance."

"Harold's already doing that," Jake said. "I thought Mr. Becker was knocked out, too, and we needed one for *him*. Mr. Becker? You hurt bad?"

"Crazy man," Mr. Becker muttered. "Knocked me right flat, him and that miserable cur of a dog."

"Who?" Jake and I said together.

It was as if Mr. Becker didn't even hear us. He had a purple lump rising on his forehead; he touched it, winced, and finally seemed to come out of his stupor when the manager, Harold, came up the stairs from the first floor.

"I got an ambulance coming," he said. "What in tarnation happened? How'd that fool dog get loose?"

Jake told him why George had been left lying in front of Magda's door. "She was coming right upstairs from Mrs. Albertoni's, and we couldn't put the dog inside because Magda had the key."

"Ought to get rid of that animal," Mr. Becker said firmly. "He's a menace. He might have killed me. I hope he taught that feller a lesson, sneaking around in here."

"What feller?" Harold asked, scowling.

"Feller that dog went after. The man came tearing down the stairs like I wasn't even in the way, that animal growling and snapping at him. They both plowed right into me."

"Who was it?" Jake asked. He had hold of George now, and the bulldog had quieted down except for panting so hard I was afraid he'd have a heart attack.

Harold worked his way past us, and knelt beside Magda and checked her pulse, then glanced back at Mr. Becker. "Well? Who was it?"

"How do I know who it was?" Mr Becker snarled, gently probing the lump, which was getting bigger and more purple by the moment. "I told you. Some stranger. Sneaking around in here. Who knows what he was after? Hadn't been for that ugly little beast he might have broken into somebody's apartment, and who knows what he'd have done then. In broad daylight, yet. Nobody's safe anymore, even in their own building."

A stranger.

My eyes met Jake's. "George's not all bad," Jake said mildly. "He ran him off. Tore a piece out of him, too, I think. A piece of his clothes, anyway. When I grabbed George, he dropped a mouthful of what looks like a man's slacks."

He dug into his pocket and produced a torn scrap of gray cloth.

"He'd made it at least to the third floor without being noticed," Mr. Becker said. "The elevator was already in use, so I decided not to wait for it to get back down to me. And I was almost to the second floor when I got run over sure as if I'd stepped out into the middle of Broadway. Where's that ambulance? Is that woman breathing?"

"Yes, but she's knocked out. We're going to have to start locking the lobby door during the day, too," Harold said, "even if it is inconvenient for some people. Jake, run out and flag down that ambulance, I hear 'em coming. Make sure they don't waste no time. Magda needs a doctor right away."

Jake handed George over to me before he ran. I wasn't sure I could hold the dog if he decided he wanted to leave, but he seemed content to sit beside me, his sides heaving in and out after his recent exercise.

The siren died, and feet pounded toward us. Two young men pushed past us with a stretcher to get to Magda and knelt beside her. Harold looked grumpily at me and George.

"Shut him up somewhere," the old man said.

"I can't put him in Magda's apartment because the door's locked," I said. "And I can't put him in our place because he'd tear it apart trying to get at Clancy."

"Who in tarnation is Clancy?" Mr. Becker asked, but nobody paid any attention to him. George had decided he didn't like the paramedics, either; and if Jake hadn't come back to help hold him, the dog would probably have knocked us all down the stairs.

"Shut *up*, George," I said desperately, and we both hung on to keep him from attacking the men, who were carefully lifting his mistress onto the stretcher.

To my relief Magda groaned when they moved her. It wasn't easy maneuvering on the stairway, and it was decided everyone but the paramedics and Magda would go down to get out of the way so she could be carried to the ambulance.

George didn't want anybody to take her anywhere, and there was a brief scuffle when Harold finally got into the act to get the dog under control. As the medics drove away with Magda, Harold jerked the ring of keys off his belt and poked it at Jake.

"They're labeled. Lock him up in her place. Mr. Becker, I'm going along to the hospital to make sure Magda's took care of. You better come along and let them check you over, too."

"I'm all right," Mr. Becker protested, but by this time I guess everybody else in the apartment house was gathered in the lobby, and they all insisted that Harold was right. While Harold went to get his car—George was whining and straining to get out the front door but he wasn't so frantic once the ambulance was out of sight—Jake asked Mr. Becker what the stranger had looked like.

"How the deuce do I know?" Mr. Becker said crossly. "I hardly even saw him before he barreled into me, him and that crazy dog. Knocked me right off my feet, slammed me into the wall, like to split my head open. They shouldn't allow dogs in this place."

"He kept the guy from getting in and doing whatever he intended to do," Jake observed. "Of course, maybe he was just a salesman or somebody like that."

"Anybody expecting a visitor?" Mr. Becker glared at the tenants standing out in the lobby. Nobody answered. "Well, he wasn't carrying anything that looked like a salesman. Only a briefcase, and he dropped that."

Jake look startled "He did? Where?"

"I'm sitting on it. The first time the dog bit him, I think, at the same time as he bowled me over, it got knocked out of his hand." Mr. Becker squirmed around and extracted a flat black leather case, wincing again as he moved. "Maybe there's something in it that tells who he is."

A thin young woman with dark hair, carrying a baby in her arms and with several more small children clinging to her, cleared her throat. "I hope he's not someone who'll sue Magda because her dog bit him. She only has her Social Security."

"If he was up to no good, he won't be suing anyone." Mr. Becker handed the briefcase over to Jake. "There's Harold with the car. I believe I will go see a doctor after all. I wouldn't be surprised if I have a concussion."

Several people moved to help him as he staggered toward the front door. The rest of the tenants began to disperse. Jake shoved the briefcase at me when George attempted to follow Mr. Becker, whining again. It took both of Jake's hands to hold him.

"Come on," Jake said. "Let's get in the elevator with the Albertonis. George will be easier to control there than on the stairs."

Mrs. Albertoni was the dark-haired lady with the children. There wasn't room for all of us in the elevator, so I took the stairs, the briefcase slapping against my leg as I ran.

The elevator had to pause to unload the Albertonis on the second floor, so I was waiting to meet it when the door slid open on the third. George dragged Jake out into the hallway. He was looking kind of bedraggled. Jake, I mean, not George.

"Get the keys out of my pocket, will you?" Jake asked. "Unlock Magda's door before this dog pulls my arms the rest of the way out of their sockets. The keys are labeled."

Once he was released, George whined and ran around the apartment, sniffing.

"He's looking for Magda," Jake said, flexing his shoulders. "I never knew how strong he is."

Guilt swamped me. "I hope she's not badly hurt. Do you think so?"

"I don't know. She was moving her head after they picked her up, so her neck isn't broken, but something else might be. People her age don't heal very fast when they break bones. She isn't here, George, but she'll be back. You'll just have to wait for her."

"It was Clancy's fault," I said. "She was being very careful on the stairs, and I think she'd have been okay if Clancy hadn't got tangled up in her feet. If Joanie hadn't let Clancy loose—"

"She probably couldn't hang on to him any better than I was doing with George. At least Clancy's small enough to pick up without killing yourself. Let's open the briefcase and see what's in it."

It wasn't locked. And it had nothing in it at all.

I stared into it, puzzled. "Why would a salesman be carrying around an empty briefcase?" I wondered aloud.

Jake took the case and checked all the compartments again. "I doubt if he *was* a salesman. There's a sign on the front door that says No Soliciting." And then he added, as if I were too stupid to know what that meant, "That means salesmen aren't allowed."

It didn't seem worth getting indignant about.

"What was he, then? Do you think he . . . had something to do with . . . my dad being missing?"

"Maybe. We don't see many strangers in this building unless they come to visit somebody, and nobody said they were expecting anyone. But it's obvious why the guy was carrying an empty case."

"Why?" I demanded, because it wasn't obvious to *me*.

Jake's eyes were gray and very serious. "Because," he said, "he expected to use the case to carry something away with him when he left."

It *was* obvious once he'd said it. I stared at him, my mouth suddenly dry. "What?" I asked.

"Who knows? Something small enough to fit in a briefcase. Money, jewelry, papers. Something he didn't want to carry in his hand, where people would see it."

George made a piteous sound and pushed his pug nose against my hand. Automatically, I scratched behind his ears and said, "It'll be all right, George." I hoped I wasn't lying.

"Maybe," Jake said thoughtfully, "whoever caused all the bloodshed in your apartment left something behind. Something that would be a clue to whatever went on there. Maybe he had to leave in a hurry, but when he remembered it he had to come back and get it."

It gave me a creepy feeling to think of some stranger—the man I'd "dreamed" about, or a different one?—coming back to the apartment to search for something—while Joanie and I were there by ourselves.

Did he have a key? Or had he intended to break in?

The shadowy figure who had stood over me had a key, I thought. My chest felt tight and it was hard to breathe.

"He could have been heading for another apartment," Jake said. "But I'm betting he wasn't. Not much excitement goes on in this place except when Magda and Harold get in a shouting match about George getting loose and tearing up the curtains at the front window while he's trying to look out. I've lived here since I was six years old and nothing like blood all over an apartment ever happened before. So what do you say we go across the hall and see if we can find whatever the guy might have been looking for?"

George didn't want to be left behind; he scratched on the inside of the door when we shut it in his face, and barked halfheartedly, but there wasn't much else we could do with him.

Joanie, holding Clancy in her arms, was standing at the window that opened onto the fire escape and the alley. She turned around with apprehension on her face.

"Is Magda dead?"

"No, but they took her to the hospital. And Mr. Becker went just to be checked, but I think *he's* all right. How come Clancy got loose? It was his fault Magda fell." I was sorry the minute I said it, because it sounded like I was blaming Joanie for letting the cat loose, and I knew he was hard to hang on to if he didn't want to be held.

Joanie was subdued. "I know. He just leaped away from me. When will we know about Magda?"

"When Harold comes home, I guess. He'll know. We don't know exactly what happened. George was loose, waiting by Magda's door for her to get up here from Mrs. Albertoni's, and he attacked some strange guy who was coming up the stairs. They knocked Mr. Becker down, maybe gave him a concussion, and then Clancy tripped Magda."

Joanie nodded, and Clancy rubbed his head under her chin as she hugged him. "I saw the man."

For a minute I didn't think I'd heard her right.

"The man George attacked?" Jake asked, incredulous.

"Yeah. I'm pretty sure it was him. He was limping, and his pants were torn."

"How did you see him?" I demanded. "*I* didn't see him!"

"In the alley," Joanie said, tilting her head toward the window. "He came running along the alley and got into a car right after I came back to the apartment. He was in a hurry to get away."

Jake took a step toward her. "What kind of car?"

Joanie shrugged. "I don't know what kind. A big silvery gray one. Elegant, Mom would have called it. He left in a hurry, anyway."

"Did you see the license number?" I asked eagerly, moving to look out the window as if I might see something, even though she'd already said the man had gone.

"No. I never even thought to look, but I probably couldn't have read it, anyway. I'm too far up. But I think there's another man down there yet."

Jake joined us at the window, pulling aside the curtain to see better. "Where? What's he doing?"

"He's kind of back in the shadows. You can't see him very plain," Joanie explained. "He went around the corner at the back of the building next door, beyond where the dumpster is. He just stood there, almost out of sight, when the other one limped to his car and drove away."

"How do you know he's still there?" I asked. There was no one in sight now.

"I saw him go around there," Joanie said. "I didn't see him come out."

"Maybe there's another way out," I said, but immediately Jake shook his head.

"Not if he went behind the building. He'd have to come out into the alley to get to a street in either direction. What did this one look like?"

"I only saw his back. He just looked ordinary. Dark slacks and a blue shirt, I think. He had dark hair."

"What's going on?" I said, feeling my heart thudding in my chest. "Look!"

Because right then something—someone— moved in the shadows next to the building. Moved—a figure looking up at our building—then withdrew again into the dimness.

Jake dropped the curtain. He'd seen the figure, too. "He's still there. And he doesn't want to be noticed." He continued to try to peer through the filmy material of the curtains. "We don't want him to know we're watching, or he may stay hidden."

He looked at Joanie. "Open the window and put the cat outside on the fire escape. If the guy's watching, he'll think that's all the action is, just putting the cat out. He probably won't be suspicious of that."

So Joanie put Clancy outside. We left the window open, but all we could hear was a car going by on the street out front, a baby crying somewhere.

We stood there, behind the curtains, and waited for the man in the shadows to move again.

9

It probably wasn't more than five minutes that we stood by the window, watching through the blur of the curtains. It seemed much longer.

The sunlight out there was so bright that the glare was hard to look into. That made the shadows darker by contrast, and I couldn't even tell that the wall of the adjoining building was built of brick within the shadows.

We had put Clancy out on the fire escape, but instead of running up to the next floor, he turned around on the window ledge, batting at the curtains as if trying to come back in.

Joanie said, "He'll snag them."

Jake stopped her from touching them. "No, leave him alone. We don't want to spook whoever's down there. It'll attract attention if he sees any movement up here, but I shouldn't think he'd pay any attention to the cat. Wait! There he is!"

I could hardly make out his figure until he finally stepped directly into the brilliant sun. He glanced up and down the alley, then swept his gaze over our building, before he turned and walked briskly through the alley toward the next street behind our apartment.

I drew in a sharp breath, and Joanie said uncertainly, "Is that Dad?"

"It is, isn't it?" Jake said. "It looks like him. He's got a beard."

"We never saw him with a beard," I said slowly, "but he's built like Dad. Tall, and with wide shoulders."

"He looks like the guy I've seen going in and out of this apartment," Jake observed, as Clancy finally came in the window.

"Why would he be hiding out there, if it's Dad?" I wondered aloud.

"Watching the guy George took after when he tried to come up the stairs. The one Joanie says parked a silvery gray car out there."

"What's going on, anyway? If it was Dad, why doesn't he come home instead of skulking around in the alley? Why did he call in sick where he works? If that's him, he sure didn't look like there was anything wrong with him."

And he obviously wasn't dead, I realized in relief. But I couldn't imagine what was going on. "I wish I'd had a better look at the figure I saw in my dream—or what I thought was a dream," I said. "I don't know if he had a beard or not. If it was Dad, why would he leave without waking me up or leaving a note or something? Why would he stay away when he knows we're here?"

We didn't have any answers, of course. Jake thought of some possibilities, though.

"Maybe the guy in the silver car is looking for him, and he doesn't want to be found. Or he's afraid of the guy for some reason."

I felt the frown lines forming between my eyebrows. "I don't remember Dad being afraid of anybody. Ever. And why would he be? I mean, Dad's an accountant, a bookkeeper. He wouldn't be a threat to anybody, not so a guy would come after him."

Jake thought about that, sinking onto one end of the couch, where Clancy immediately leaped into his lap. Jake absently stroked him, and I could hear the purr from halfway across the room.

"A bookkeeper. Hmm. Maybe he found something in the books that wasn't supposed to be there."

I stared at him. "Like what? Usually the books list the money that comes into a business, and what it goes out for, and how much there is left over."

Jake nodded. "Right. So if something came in that wasn't supposed to—or went out, that wasn't supposed to—a bookkeeper might discover it. And maybe whoever juggled the books wouldn't want him to know about it."

I scowled. "Why would they hire a bookkeeper and try to keep something a secret from him? Besides, he's working for a *union*. How much money would they handle, anyway? They don't *sell* anything."

"True. They don't handle a product. But I think they might handle quite a lot of money. Union dues, you know. I don't know what the money is spent on, but I've heard my dad gripe about how much his dues are."

That distracted me a little. "Does he belong to the Manufacturers Consolidated Trust?"

"No. He's in the electricians' union, and he has to pay the dues or he can't work a union job. Oh, crumb, listen!"

There were two doors and the width of the hall between us, but there was no mistaking George's voice. He had begun to howl.

"He's lonesome," Joanie said.

Clancy stopped purring and lifted his head, then jumped out of Jake's lap, stalking toward the door.

We listened uneasily to George's cries of distress.

"I hope Harold brings Magda home when he comes," Jake said. "I think I'd better go get George, put a leash on him, and take him out in the back alley, the way Magda does several times a day. She can't walk very far, but he *has* to go out."

"We'll go with you," I offered quickly. "Maybe somebody left some clues out there."

Nobody had, though. At least we didn't find any.

Dad's car was there, but it was locked. We couldn't see anything inside of any interest.

George sniffed and smelled pretty much everything before he did his business. Then we walked him around the block, which he seemed to like, and when we came around to the front of the building we met Harold and Mr. Becker, coming home.

There was no sign of Magda.

"They decided to keep her overnight," Harold informed us. "No broken bones, but she was pretty shook up. If she feels okay in the morning, she can come home, but she'll probably want pain medication for a few days. Clumsy old fool, she knows better than to tackle the stairs. That's why we got an elevator."

I felt compelled to stick up for her. "It wasn't her fault she fell. It was Clancy's. He got tangled up in her feet and tripped her."

Harold grunted as he helped Mr. Becker up the steps. "Lucky we didn't kill off half the tenants. Mr. Becker's got a mild concussion, and he's kind of wobbly. You kids better take care of the dog. I ain't got time to do it."

I waited until they'd gone inside before I said what I'd been thinking. "Maybe you'd better keep him, Jake. He'll probably howl all night if we leave him alone in Magda's place."

Jake was startled. "Hey, I can't take him to my place! The only thing my dad hates worse than a cat is a dog! He'd throw me out if I brought George to our place."

Suddenly a cat that wasn't paying attention to us moved across the street, and George threw his whole body into a dive at him. Jake got dragged off the curb before he was able to haul back on the leash enough to stop him, and then George barked his frustration as the cat scrambled up the nearest tree.

"Well, we can't take him," I protested. "Not with Clancy in the apartment, too. They'd kill each other."

It was a stalemate. We stood there looking at one another.

"Maybe," Joanie said hesitantly, "we could shut George in the kitchen and Clancy in the bedroom, so they couldn't get at each other."

It sounded kind of risky. If either of them squeezed past us when we opened a door, they'd probably demolish the place before we could get them under control. But nobody could think of a better plan.

In the elevator, on the way up to the third floor, Jake said, "Let's see if we can figure out what the guy in the silver car intended to carry away in that briefcase."

A lump formed in my throat. I hated to think it was all connected to Dad's apartment, even though common sense told me it must be. "In Dad's apartment, you mean?"

The look he gave me was almost pitying. "Well, yeah. I mean, that's where all the blood is. It's where your dad's missing from. And it's where you 'dreamed' some guy walked in on you, using a key, and looked at you but didn't leave a note or stick around long enough to say hello, and after he was gone so was the picture that had been on top of the bookcase. So, yeah, I think if the guy was coming back for something, it would be in your apartment."

I guess I'd known all that, but when he summed it up that way it sounded . . . ominous.

The elevator stopped, and the doors slid creakily open. As George jerked him out onto the third floor, Jake looked back at me and asked, "Is it okay if I come help you search?"

"Sure," I agreed at once, though I didn't really want to believe this was all connected to Dad and as dangerous as I suspected it could be. "Look, doesn't it seem to you that there are *two* men involved here, and they're not necessarily working together? I mean"—Joanie and I followed him down the corridor to the apartment—"if that was Dad in the alley, he seemed to be *watching* someone—probably the guy in the silver car, the one George took after—didn't he? Not as if they were working together?"

I'd forgotten Clancy.

He had been dozing on the back of the couch. When George lumbered through the doorway, stretching his leash as far ahead of Jake as he could, Clancy and the dog became aware of each other at the same moment.

George lunged, jerking the leash out of Jake's hand, and with a screech of outrage Clancy leaped onto the top of the bookcase and then up onto the nearest curtain rod; a moment later the rod, curtains and all, came down on top of George, and Clancy streaked for the nearest open window and disappeared.

Luckily the opening wasn't big enough to let the bulldog through or he'd have been out on the fire escape, too. I helped Jake untangle George from the curtains and heard Joanie say, "Uh-oh. They're torn."

And the rod was bent, too. Jake straightened it out without comment. The bent place hardly showed when we rehung everything, and we arranged the folds so you could hardly see the tear unless you were looking for it.

"I don't know if this is going to work," I said, glaring at George.

"Lock him in the kitchen," Jake said absently. "Come on, let's check this place out. Whatever it is we're looking for, it's small enough to fit in a briefcase."

Actually, it didn't take very long to go over the whole apartment. Dad hadn't been there long enough to accumulate very many belongings. There wasn't much furniture; we looked under and behind everything, just in case. And we turned pockets inside out, went through mostly empty dresser drawers, and opened every door and drawer in the kitchen. We discovered peanut butter and crackers, and remembered we hadn't had any lunch, so we sat at the table and ate those with the last of the canned pop. It made me nervous to see the supplies shrinking so fast; I had hardly any money left to buy more.

George whined and scratched on the other side of the door when we shut him in the kitchen, but we ignored him. He just couldn't be trusted to run around loose. "We'd better go over to Magda's and get him some dog food," I said, so we went across the hall and filled a paper bag. I paused, looking at the cookie jar on the counter. "I wonder how long Magda's going to be in the hospital? I mean, those cookies won't stay fresh for very long, will they?"

Jake looked in at them, selected one, and bit into it. "We might as well take them, too. And maybe anything else that won't keep very long."

I felt a little guilty about helping ourselves. Dad would see that she was repaid, though, I was sure. And we needed to stretch our groceries as far as we could.

George was eager to dive into the dry dog food,

and that time when we closed the kitchen door he didn't scratch at it, only whined a little.

"What are we going to do now?" Joanie asked, smiling when Clancy cautiously reentered the room. He surveyed the place thoroughly from the safety of the window ledge before he made his way to Joanie's lap, switching his tail as if in warning to any fool dog that was unwise enough to pop out at him.

"We could call the hospital back," Jake suggested, "and see if they found out your dad's with a patient. If that *wasn't* him we saw in the alley," he amended.

It didn't seem likely that there were two big, dark-bearded men involved in this case—I was thinking of it as a *case* by this time—but it was something to do.

It was wasted effort. Nobody at the hospital knew anything about a patient named Steve Rakosi. They had even asked over the intercom system if anyone by that name was among the visitors, but there'd been no response. I hung up, discouraged.

Joanie was holding Clancy on her stomach as she sprawled on the end of the couch, making him purr. "Vickie, are we just going to stay stuck in this place until Dad comes? This is boring."

"Boring," I agreed. "And kind of scary, too. I wish we'd had a chance to read that last letter Dad sent to Mom. Maybe he explained some of this stuff."

"We shouldn't have come," Joanie said soberly, "without talking to Dad first."

"Well, that's easy to figure out," I said crossly, "now that we're here and everything's so screwed up. The question is, what do we do now?"

"Wait," Jake said. He sounded like Gram. *Don't be*

so impatient, Victoria. Everything will happen when it's supposed to. Just wait.

Behind the kitchen door, George gave a half-hearted bark, and I turned my head and spoke to him automatically. "Shut up, George."

The top of the bookcase was in my line of sight, and my gaze lingered there, though I wasn't sure why. It was just an empty top board with a faint trace of dust on the wood.

And then it hit me, and I wondered why I hadn't noticed before.

I must have made a sound because Jake looked at me questioningly.

"The pipe," I said, feeling strangled. "There was a pipe, and now it's gone, too."

10

"What are you upset about?" Joanie asked, puzzled. "What difference does it make if the pipe's gone?"

"Because, stupid, it means somebody took it! Just like the picture."

"You mean Dad took it?"

"Maybe! But he didn't make any contact with us, if he did. And whose blood was all over in here? There's something *wrong*, Joanie! Dad's in some kind of bad trouble!"

"I wish we'd stayed home," she said, her lower lip coming out the way it did when she wasn't getting her own way.

"I didn't want you to come," I reminded her. "I *said* you were too little. And what good would it have done to have stayed home? We couldn't be any help to Dad that way."

She screwed up her face in concentration. "Are we helping Dad?"

Jake answered that. "Probably not very much so far. But maybe we could. I can't figure out why he's ignoring you, though. He's got to know you're here, doesn't he? Unless it was someone else who used the key to get in and stood there looking at you. It would sure help if you'd noticed if he had a beard or not."

By this time I was so frustrated I snapped at him, too. "Well, excuse me for not waking up enough to realize there was someone really here, and that it wasn't a dream! I suppose you'd have done better!"

Jake laughed. "It's not my fault. Don't take it out on me. It's too bad George didn't tear enough of a chunk out of that guy with the briefcase to slow him down a little. Maybe we'd have figured out who he was and what he wanted."

I stared at the door that we didn't have a key to. "If we give Harold's keys back, we can lock it from the inside, but we can't lock it behind us if we leave. And even inside we're not safe in here if somebody besides Dad has a key."

"Why?" Joanie asked. "Why wouldn't we be safe? What would he do to us?"

"How do I know? Something happened to *some-body* in here, that's for sure. I just don't want anything else to make anybody bleed. How are we going to sleep if we have to be afraid the guy is going to come back and we can't keep him out?"

"You can keep him out," Jake said. "Fasten the chain. Even if he has a key he won't be able to get past the chain. And if it will make you feel better, move the recliner over against the door. If anybody shoves on it, you'll probably hear it and wake up."

"Oh, goodie! Then I can die of fright." I stared at him as if it were *his* fault, even while I could hear Gram in my imagination. *Stop blaming other people for your problems, Victoria. It's a sign of immaturity.* The trouble was, I didn't feel very mature right then. I was worried and scared. Not even having Jake around helped much.

He continued to be unhelpful when he said, "Maybe you ought to just go back home and let your dad handle it, whatever it is."

"We *can't* go home, we spent all our money just getting down here, and we don't have tickets to go back. And if Dad's in real trouble, it's our duty to help him, isn't it? Wouldn't you feel that way if it was *your* dad?"

Jake considered that. "I'm not sure. My old man's meaner than a rattlesnake. I doubt if he'd need any help." He held up a hand against the expression forming on my face. "Just kidding. I think. Anyway, your dad's a grown man. Chances are he can take care of himself."

Maybe. Maybe not. All that hastily cleaned-up blood bothered me a lot. I wished I knew whose blood it was. If it was Dad who'd been injured, apparently he hadn't been killed, but why wouldn't he acknowledge that Joanie and I were there? It didn't make sense.

I was as annoyed with Jake as I was with my little sister, but it was kind of a jolt when he announced that he was going home. "I've got some homework to do. I've got an essay due on Monday," he said. "And my dad said if I didn't wash the dishes that have stacked up by tonight, he'd ground me for a week. He might do it."

My stomach tightened. Somehow I'd taken it for

granted that he wasn't going to leave us alone in this peculiar situation.

"Are you just going to skip school next week?" he asked.

"I guess so. We're sure not going to start here."

Jake stood up, but he lingered. "Doesn't anybody care if you don't go?"

I shrugged. "I didn't ask. It just seemed more important to come here and see Dad."

"Any special reason?" Jake wondered. "I mean, in a couple of weeks school will be out for the summer. And apparently your dad wasn't expecting you."

It wasn't really any of his business, and from the tone of his voice I suspected he'd be critical. Still, he had more or less befriended us.

Before I could decide what, if anything, to tell him, Joanie blurted, "She had a big fight with Gram."

"Ahh." Jake nodded in understanding. "If I took off to see my ma whenever my old man and I have a big fight, I might as well move out and back in with her in the first place. She says Dad and I don't get along because we're too much alike." He looked rueful. "I hope she's wrong, because I don't really want to be as mean as he is."

Joanie let herself be diverted from the issues of what was wrong here and what we were going to do about it. "Your mom doesn't live with you?"

"No. My folks split about a year ago. Mom moved over to Merced and got a job. She lives near my grandparents, and except for missing me she says it's a much easier life than squabbling with my dad all the time."

Clancy, who had been dozing on Joanie's lap, suddenly leaped down and stalked to the window. Obligingly, Jake pulled the curtains aside for him to reach the sill, but instead of letting them fall back into place he hesitated there.

"What?" I demanded immediately, because there was something about the way he went so still that alerted me.

"Joanie," he said softly, as if he might be heard beyond this room, "is this the same car you saw, that the guy got into after George tore his pants?"

She moved to stand beside him, and I went to look over her shoulder, too. A silvery gray sedan was just rolling to a stop in the alley.

"A new Crown Victoria," Jake noted. "Nice car. Not the kind we usually have parked in the alley."

We were looking down on it and we couldn't make out the driver, or if there was more than one person in the car. And nobody got out.

Instinctively my gaze shifted to the shadowy part of the building, where the bearded man had hidden earlier, but as far as I could tell, there was no one there now. The sun had changed position so the shadows were different, and it was hot and still out there. Nothing moved.

Why should that have sent a shiver down my spine?

I didn't know, but the hair continued to prickle on the back of my neck after Jake had left and Joanie and I were alone in the apartment.

I racked my brain to think what I ought to be doing to help my dad, though I was mad because he couldn't even be bothered to let us know he knew we were here.

Behind the kitchen door, George made snuffling noises, then barked.

I sighed before I remembered that I hadn't given him any water, only the dog food. "Hold Clancy," I told Joanie, "just in case this fool dog gets past me."

He didn't, though. I felt guilty when he lapped up the whole bowl of water and looked at me, panting and dripping, waiting for me to refill the dish. He was halfway through the second bowlful when Joanie spoke from the living room.

"Vic. He's back!"

"Who?" I asked, slipping away from George and closing the door behind me as I joined her. Joanie was standing at the window, craning her head to look down into the alley.

"See, over there! In the shadows, again."

It was hard to see anything in the shadow; at first the contrast between there and the sunlit alley was so great that it was like looking into blackness. And then my eyes adjusted a little and I could make out the figure in the indentation toward the rear of the opposite building. No details, just a tall, dark shape.

I drew in a deep breath, suddenly so frustrated I felt like gnashing my teeth.

"Did you get a good look at him before he slipped into that place? Was it Dad?"

Joanie rocked Clancy and rubbed her chin on his head. "I didn't see him coming. I don't know. Does he have a beard?"

It was impossible to tell. Everything was impossible, including staying here much longer if Dad didn't come home and get some more groceries.

The idea flashed into my mind, and I didn't even stop to consider the probable consequences.

"Stay here, and put the chain on the door as soon as I leave," I told her.

She turned away from the window, startled. "Where are you going?"

"Down there. Down there to find out what the heck is going on."

Her mouth sagged open. "How are you going to do that?"

"I'm going to walk right up to one or the other of those guys—or maybe both of them—and ask. This is crazy, sitting here waiting, doing nothing."

She squeezed Clancy until he resisted. He yowled, leaped away from her, and hid behind the couch. "What if . . . the men are dangerous?"

"Dad's not likely to be dangerous, is he? And if the other one does anything, well, you've got a telephone here. Call the police. The address is on that phone bill on the desk."

Joanie looked panicky. "But I can't see all of the alley, Vickie! What if I can't tell what's happening?"

"Go out on the fire escape and look."

I was already taking the chain off the door.

"But then he'll know we're watching him!" Joanie protested. "I thought we were trying not to have anybody see us!"

"Dad already knows we're here, it seems like. And if the other guy is doing anything that you need to call the cops for, it won't matter."

Joanie moistened her lips. For once she wasn't arguing about being left behind. "What if the guy in the car is a cop? What if he's after Dad?"

"A cop? Why would a cop be after Dad?" But I knew even before Joanie came up with her own answer.

"Because of all the blood. Somebody got hurt, didn't he? Right here in this apartment."

"How would the police know that?" I scoffed, even as the very idea made my chest feel tight. "As far as we know, they haven't been here. Nobody knows about the blood except us. And Jake. Besides, we're pretty sure the guy in the car is the one who tried to come up the stairs with an empty briefcase, to take something away. Why would he do that if he were a cop? He wouldn't have run away just because George ripped his pants, either." I jerked open the door. "Remember, put the chain back on as soon as I'm gone. Then watch out the window. Dial 911 if it looks like I'm in trouble."

"I know enough to call 911," Joanie said indignantly as I closed the door with her still talking. "Vickie, I hope he doesn't shoot you."

"Why would anybody shoot me?" I asked through the door, then walked quickly toward the elevator.

Still, I couldn't help hoping that nobody would. Shoot me, I mean.

11

The elevator was in use, apparently. At any rate it didn't come after I pushed the button, so I gave up after a minute or two and took the stairs.

When I reached the area where Magda and Mr. Becker had fallen my stomach tightened, but I kept on going. I was scared, but I had to do *something* besides sit around waiting.

Two elderly ladies were standing in the lobby, visiting. And the elevator door was in the process of closing on a passenger who didn't look in my direction.

"Dad!" I yelped, startled, but the doors went shut, and I heard the *whir* as the car began to move. "Darn!"

The old women stopped talking and looked at me.

"Did you see the man who just got on the elevator?" I demanded.

One of them looked at me the way Gram does—as if she'd just bitten into a pickle—but the other one spoke politely. "Yes, we saw him. The tenant in 3B, I think. I don't recall his name, but he has a black beard. I've seen him going in and out before."

I started to turn back toward the stairs, knowing that he'd probably get to the third floor before I would, even on that slow old elevator, and then I stopped, transfixed. I always liked that word, in books, and I've never had a chance to use it before, but it fits.

Transfixed. I watched a man in a gray suit come up the walk—from the direction of the alley where the silvery car was parked—and I froze.

He was carrying a briefcase, and I *knew*.

I spoke hastily to the old ladies. "Do you know that man who's coming in?"

They looked first at me, as if I were crazy, and then at the stranger. The pickle lady shrugged. "*No.*" The nicer one shook her head. "Probably a salesman. They're not supposed to bother the tenants, but they do."

I forgot to say thank you. I spun, just as the stranger reached for the door, and raced up the stairs.

Behind me, I heard the nice lady ask sweetly, "Are you looking for someone in particular, sir?"

"I know where he lives," the man said.

And then, to my horror, I heard his feet on the stairs behind me.

I ran for all I was worth, careless of how much noise I was making. I wanted to get to Dad before the man with the briefcase reached the third floor.

I was puffing when I got to the landing and ran

out of the stairwell. A quick glance backward showed the stranger hadn't caught up to me yet, but I heard his feet, measured, purposeful.

The corridor was carpeted, so I hadn't heard the footsteps there, but the elevator had beaten me, and there was the man I'd glimpsed from the lobby, walking toward the front of the building, getting out his keys.

"Dad!" I called, trotting toward him just as I sensed the other man emerging from the stairwell. "Dad, it's me, Vickie!"

He twisted the key in the lock before he turned to face me, and by that time the man with the briefcase was right behind me. His voice was so close that it sent a shiver down my back, even though I was not absolutely sure why he scared me so much.

"Rakosi," he barked in an authoritative tone.

The tall, bearded man stuck his keys back in his pocket and waited, one hand on the doorknob.

His eyes met mine and I felt the shock wash over me in a cold wave, because they were blue, not brown like Dad's.

The man with the beard, carrying a key to Dad's apartment, was a complete stranger.

Yet the *other* stranger had called him Rakosi.

I felt numb, paralyzed. I was scared stiff.

What was going on?

"Yes? Oh, Mr. . . . Zeeman, isn't it?"

The man with the beard glanced at the one who'd climbed the stairs behind me, and then at me. His gaze bored right into me, and though I'd never seen him before, I had the strong feeling that he was sending me an urgent message.

Only I didn't have the faintest idea what it was.

His lips moved in a sort of smile. "Yes, Vickie," he said as if he were really Dad, "go on inside. I'll be in in a minute, I need to talk to Mr. Zeeman. He's the president of the company I work for."

He twisted the knob, but the door only opened an inch or so. I managed to speak, just barely.

"I think Joanie's got the chain on; she'll have to take it off the hook."

"Uh . . . Joanie. Yeah," the man pretending to be Dad said. He rapped on the door. "Joanie! Let us in!"

My mind raced. Should I tell her to do it, or to call the police? I didn't understand anything, and though I sensed danger all around me, I couldn't tell which of the men it was coming from.

Danger.

Yes, definitely danger. Where was Dad? This bearded man wasn't him, which meant Dad *could* have been the one who got hurt and left the blood all over the place.

He'd answered to Dad's name, and Joanie was still safe, behind the door, and Jake had gone back up to his own apartment to write an essay. And here I was, standing in the hallway with two strangers, not knowing which of them—if either—to trust.

Joanie's voice, wavering enough to let me know she was scared, too, came from the other side of the door. "Who—who is it?"

The blue-eyed stranger looked me straight in the face and said clearly, "It's Dad, Joanie. Let us in."

And the message was there in his eyes for me. *Pretend I'm him. Pretend I'm your dad. Don't give me away.*

I swallowed hard and cleared my throat and spoke toward the door. "Let us in, Joanie."

We heard the chain rattle, and she opened the door, relief on her face. Before she could get a good look at the man right behind me, I pushed inside, and whispered softly, "Don't say anything. Keep still."

She was startled, but for once in her life she did what I said without arguing. At least for a few seconds.

I was blocking the view from the man called Zeeman, which was a good thing because I saw her face when she realized that the bearded man wasn't who he was pretending to be. She gave me an anxious, questioning glance, and I spoke loudly to cover her voice in case she said something stupid.

Until I figured out what was going on, it seemed safest to go along with the fake Steve Rakosi. The hair was prickling on the back of my neck and on my bare arms, and my mouth was so dry it was a wonder my voice worked.

"Keep Clancy away from Dad. He'll get white hair all over his pants."

She looked at me as if I'd lost my mind, but again she didn't say anything to give the guy away. She backed out of my way, holding the cat against her chest, and even if she stayed quiet, Mr. Zeeman was going to know something was wrong if he got a look at her face.

Behind me, the door was still ajar, and I heard the imposter say, "What was it you needed, Mr. Zeeman? I'll be back in the office on Monday, if it can wait that long."

"I don't think it can." The voice was deadly, very low, like something out of one of those old black-and-white Humphrey Bogart movies Dad always loved. I'd enjoyed getting goose bumps sitting beside Dad to watch them, but I didn't feel good about the ones I had now. It was different when the menace was real instead of on the screen. "I believe you have some papers that belong to me, Rakosi."

"Papers? No, sir, I don't think I do."

I turned enough to see my "dad" standing in the doorway, resting one hand on the knob. I couldn't see Mr. Zeeman, but I could *feel* him, just around the corner. He made me shiver.

"Maybe you picked them up by mistake," Mr. Zeeman said.

"I'm sorry, sir. I guess maybe my head's still a little fuzzy from this darned flu. I don't know what you're talking about."

Down the hall I heard the elevator door open, and there were voices. Neither man appeared to pay any attention.

"I'm talking about some papers that are missing from the office," Mr. Zeeman stated in that same low tone. "You were the last person to handle them, I think. Ralph Douglas handed them to you."

"Oh! Well, I gave all that stuff back to him, the same day. And I've been home sick, I haven't seen anybody from the office—"

"He came here, didn't he? Douglas?"

"Here? To my apartment? I don't think so"—the imposter turned his head and looked directly at me—"unless he came while I was sleeping, and one of the kids talked to him—"

What did he expect, that I was going to invent some lie when I didn't even know what they were talking about? For a guy I'd never met until a few minutes ago?

I stared at him, bewildered, and unexpectedly he smiled. "That's it. Vickie says she was the one who answered the door that first day, when I'd come home sick."

Since I hadn't said anything, and this was getting more and more bizarre, my mouth dropped open.

He grinned at me, for Mr. Zeeman's benefit, though that warning was still there in his eyes. "Yes, he was here, but I was running a fever and being sick, so he didn't stay."

"Are you saying you didn't see him?" Mr. Zeeman sounded intense.

"That's right."

"Let me talk to the girl," Mr. Zeeman said, and the next thing I knew he'd herded the imposter inside and followed him.

Joanie and I backed up to get out of the way, and I wasn't sure how long my little sister was going to keep her mouth shut. I stepped on her foot just to get her attention, and she glared at me.

"Vickie, I don't remember—"

"Of course you don't," I said quickly. "You'd gone across the hall to visit Magda, remember?"

I couldn't really have said why I was backing up the imposter. I was afraid of him, and worried about why he was pretending to be Dad. But I was more afraid of Mr. Zeeman. There was something about him I didn't like or trust a bit.

And at that moment I was pretty nervous about what was going to happen to Joanie and me.

Mr. Zeeman stared at me, and in spite of the heat of the room I broke out in a cold sweat. He smiled as if he meant to show that he was friendly, but he didn't *feel* friendly.

"Vickie, that your name? Do you remember Mr. Douglas coming here? Day before yesterday, in the evening?"

My heart tried to stop. I like to act, but only when someone else has already written the script, or I've at least been given a few clues to what is supposed to be happening so I can improvise.

I didn't know what to say. I didn't want to make up something that would trip me up as a liar. I looked uncertainly at the man who looked so much like my dad.

"It was probably right after I'd been throwing up, and then I went to sleep," he prompted.

"What time was it?" Mr. Zeeman persisted.

"I don't remember. I didn't look at the clock," I said. At least that was no lie.

I wasn't looking right into Mr. Zeeman's face. If I did, he'd probably see what a panic I was in, and he'd know for sure he wasn't getting the truth.

"Evening," the fake Steve Rakosi said. "Eight-thirty, nine maybe. I mean, I woke up about ten when I got sick again, so he was gone before that."

"And he didn't ask about the papers, Vickie?"

"He didn't ask *me*," I said, and thought about how much harder it was to lie than I'd expected. I felt as if my blood were starting to freeze and not enough of it was getting to my brain to enable me to think.

Mr. Zeeman lowered his voice and turned toward Joanie. "How about you, young lady? Did you see this visitor while you were coming or going from across the hall?"

I didn't know what Joanie was going to say, she tends to be bluntly truthful. She opened her mouth, and I felt the imposter go as rigid as I was. Even though I couldn't take my eyes off her, I knew that our questioner was tense and earnest, too.

"I never—" she started, and then all of a sudden we were saved—for a minute, anyway—when the curtains onto the fire escape billowed out and Superman flew in through the window.

12

It wasn't really Superman, of course, It was Jake. But he looked like our rescuer at a time when we really needed one.

"Hey, Vickie," he said urgently as he disentangled himself from the filmy curtains, "I saw—"

He became aware of Mr. Zeeman and the imposter and fell silent, though he forgot to close his mouth.

"Uh"—Jake bobbed his head toward the bearded man—"uh—hi, Mr. Rakosi. Um, I hope it's okay if I came down the fire escape instead of using the elevator and knocking on your front door. I waited and waited, but somebody was using the elevator, and the fire escape seemed easier."

The imposter didn't look as if he welcomed the intrusion. "It might be better to use the inside stairs," he said in a tone much like Dad might have used. "Next time."

"Uh, sure. Yes, sir," Jake said. "I didn't know there was anyone here except Vickie and Joanie. I guess . . . maybe I better come back some other time, huh?"

Mr. Zeeman was staring at him as if Jake were an unwelcome visitor. "You live upstairs?" he asked.

"Yes, sir. In 4B." Jake teetered back and forth on the balls of his feet while he decided what to do. I didn't think he really wanted to leave; he wanted to know what was happening.

"And you know the Rakosis?"

"Sure. Well, I only met Vickie and Joanie when they came to visit. Mr. Rakosi's been here for a few weeks, I guess."

Mr. Zeeman looked at each of us in turn as if he could peer into our heads and read our minds. It made me cold all the way through.

Zeeman's gaze swung back to the bearded man. "I'm sorry, Rakosi. It seems I've been misinformed. I need to do some rechecking. The missing papers are important ones that should never have left the office."

"I hope you find them, sir," my dad's almost-double said. "And I'll be back on the job Monday to help figure out where they went, if they haven't turned up before that."

Zeeman hesitated for a few seconds, scrutinizing each of us in a way that made my skin crawl. Then he nodded curtly. "Very well. I'll see you Monday morning at the office."

He closed the door behind himself as he went out, and a little of the tension seeped out of the room. Not much, but some.

For a couple of long seconds we all stood there, frozen like a bunch of little kids playing statues. I imagined Zeeman walking away, going down the stairs or in the elevator, safely away from us.

But the imposter was still there.

I filled my lungs and stared him straight in the face. "Who are you?" I demanded. "Where's my dad?"

Out of the corner of my eye I caught Jake's stunned reaction, but I didn't have time yet to deal with him.

I didn't expect the imposter's reaction. He scowled at me as if he'd like to give me a smack, instead of being grateful that I'd more or less backed him up. "You don't belong here," he said. "Get back on a bus, or a train, or however you got here, and go home."

He sounded so angry that I took a step backward, away from him. I didn't give up the offensive entirely, though. I was too worried about Dad. "Where is he?" I persisted. "Is he all right?"

"Listen, young lady. You could get me killed, and the less you know the less likely it is *you'll* get hurt. Go home."

"We can't," Joanie piped. "We don't have money for the bus tickets."

His language was shocking, and there was so much force behind the words that we had to take him seriously. Even Jake blinked, and I could feel the heat climbing into my face. The man reached into his hip pocket for his wallet, checked out its contents, and extracted several bills. He shoved them into my limp hand. "There. Go get your tickets, and go home. Today. Right now."

Jake shifted his attention to me. "Hey, what's going on? Isn't this your dad?"

"No," I said, and the man in question spoke over top of whatever Joanie was trying to say.

"You repeat that in front of the wrong person and I'm a dead man," he told me, and there was no way I could doubt that he meant it. "And maybe your dad will be, too."

"You mean so far he's okay? Where is he? Why are you here? Why do you have his keys?"

He swore again, obviously furious about having to deal with me. "Go home," he said firmly.

I'd been so scared I was shaking, but now I started to get mad. I don't know how brave I'd have been alone, but having Jake there gave me courage. "I'm not going anywhere," I told the man, curling my fingers around the money he'd handed me, "until I know about Dad."

"He's alive," was the grim reply. "If you want him to stay that way, and the rest of us, too, forget everything you've seen and heard here and go home and wait until he contacts you. Don't talk to anybody about any of this."

"Maybe we need to call the police," Jake said.

He was shriveled by the scorching glare that raked over him. "You stay out of this, whoever you are. And keep your mouth shut. I'm telling you the truth: Careless talk could cost lives, and if you know too much, the lives could even be your own. Now get out of here. You"—he fixed those blue eyes on me—"pack up your stuff and leave. There's enough money there so you can call a cab to pick you up."

Joanie's lower lip was trembling. "You're not like Daddy at all. He doesn't talk to us this way."

"He would if he were here now," the man assured us. "And I hope the next time he sees you he paddles your butts."

"Hey," Jake said, "you're asking a lot, considering that nobody knows who you are, or what's going on, or whether you're one of the good guys or the bad guys. Why should we just take your word for anything?"

"Yeah, why?" I added. I wished I could stop shaking. "Is my dad hurt? Was it him who bled all over the place? Is that why he's not here?"

For a few seconds there was no response. Then the man inhaled deeply and let out a sigh. "If you kids are typical of teenagers today, I'm sure glad I'm not raising any."

It was the most normal thing he'd said yet, and I felt braver about what I said back. "What's wrong with being concerned about our dad? How can it endanger anybody to tell us if he's hurt or what? Is somebody taking care of him?"

He hesitated, and for a moment I thought maybe he was going to answer my questions. Then he turned and walked to the desk and picked up the phone.

I tried to watch what numbers he dialed, though it was hard to be sure from where I stood. Jake was watching intently, too. I knew from his face that I'd guessed right about the Shadow Man calling the number that had left an imprint on the notepad on Dad's desk.

"Aaron Feldman here," the stranger said into the receiver. "Let me talk to Brodski." There was a brief wait, while it worked its way through my mind: he was calling the hospital where they'd said they didn't know anybody named Rakosi. My heart picked up speed.

Joanie moved close to me and leaned into my side, and I took hold of her hand, as much for my sake as hers, I guess.

"Yeah, this is Feldman," the imposter said finally. "How's he doing?"

My stomach lurched, and Joanie's fingers tightened on mine. "Dad?" she whispered.

From his expression I didn't think he got a positive answer. When he spoke again, he sounded grim. "Rakosi's kids are here. I'm sending them home, getting them out of here, but Zeeman's suspicious. And the kids want to call in the cops."

I sucked in a breath, and said, "We didn't give you away. The least you owe us for that is an explanation."

"Right," Jake agreed. Feldman ignored us, intent on someone on the other end of the line. Jake spoke again. "Come on, mister, show us some ID. Give us a reason to trust you. You can't expect Vickie and Joanie to go home without knowing if their dad's all right. *Is* it his blood all over the place?"

Feldman gave him an unfriendly look as he listened on the phone. Then he said into the receiver, "They found the bloodstains. They want an explanation. . . . Well then, go *ask* him what he wants me to do!"

There was a long silence, during which George continued to whimper and scratch on the kitchen door. The man suddenly turned in that direction and said in frustration, "What's making that racket?"

"George," I said. "He's a bulldog. He belongs to the lady across the hall. She fell down the stairs when that Mr. Zeeman came earlier, and she's in the hospital."

He didn't seem surprised at any of this. I couldn't read his expression behind the beard when he studied us without comment.

"ID," Jake prompted. "If you're a good guy, you must have ID."

"Not this trip," the man said shortly.

"Well, buddy, then unless you've got a gun and you're going to shoot all three of us, we're going to call the cops."

Air whistled from between Feldman's lips. "I almost wish I could shoot all three of you," he said flatly.

Joanie's eyes went big and round, and though I didn't think he was entirely serious, his words made my mouth dry.

There was another silence, and George whined especially piteously. I raised my voice with the order. "Shut up, George!"

I don't know why I bothered. He scratched at the door even harder, and I wondered what old Harold was going to say when he saw the damage.

Jake's gaze locked with mine, and then he took two steps toward the window. "I'm going upstairs and use my own phone," he announced.

He didn't get another step before Feldman's hand closed on his shoulder, holding him in place while he finished his phone conversation.

Jake licked his lips but I had to admire the way he refused to back off. "Unless you're going to shoot me," he said, "you can't stop me from calling." His voice only squeaked a little.

"You might tempt me," Feldman said, "if I had anything to shoot you with. Yeah, I'm still here. What'd he say?"

So we waited a little longer, while he got his orders from somebody, and then he said, "Okay," and hung up. He took his hand off Jake's shoulder.

"ID?" Jake persisted.

"It wouldn't mean a thing to you."

"Try us," Jake said.

After a hesitation that lasted only seconds, the imposter produced a wallet and flipped it open. Jake and I moved forward to look at it.

Just an ordinary driver's license, with Feldman's picture, but my eyes popped when I saw the name on it: Stavo Joseph Rakosi.

"But you're not!" I blurted. "Up close, you don't really even look like him all that much!"

"Thank you for not saying that in front of Zeeman," he said, and he sounded less annoyed with us.

I was annoyed with Jake, though, when he bent forward for a closer inspection and spoke with admiration. "Fake ID. It sure looks like the real thing. Where do you get something like that made?"

Aaron Feldman gave him a long, sober look. "There's no legal way *you're* going to get any fake ID."

"Are you a cop, then?" I asked, confused.

He hesitated, then said, "I'm a diesel mechanic."

Joanie's face screwed up in bewilderment. "What's that got to do with anything?"

"Whose blood is all over this place?" I demanded,

getting him back to the important thing. "Is it Dad's?"

Again he hesitated, and then he gestured toward the couch. "Sit down. All three of you. I can't tell you everything, but my boss said to explain enough to reassure you—and shut you up. Then you get on the bus and go home."

We sat down, and he pulled out the desk chair, turned it around to face us, and sat down, too.

"The blood," I prompted.

"The blood," he echoed, then sat there for a moment as if he couldn't think where to start.

"And Dad. He's hurt, isn't he?" My chest began to ache, waiting for his reply.

"Yes, he got hurt, but the doctors think he's going to be fine. Look, let me tell this my own way, will you?"

Joanie reached out and took my hand, and Jake's eyes were bright with interest. He could afford to be just *interested*, it wasn't *his* father.

"Your dad took a job working for a union," Aaron Feldman began finally when I was about ready to start screaming. "It was supposed to be an ordinary accounting job. Only he discovered something that he suspected meant someone was embezzling union pension funds. He wasn't sure what to do about it, so he contacted a law enforcement agency."

"The police?" Joanie asked, as Jake said, "The FBI?"

He ignored them except for scowling to indicate they should shut up and let him proceed. "The agency enlisted his help in getting proof, and everybody thought he had the perfect opportunity when he had to do some work at night, alone in the office. He 'borrowed' some of the incriminating papers of figures and brought them home, and one of our agents was going to be sent over here to do a quick appraisal of them. They figured nobody would miss them before Monday, only apparently the vice president of the union—"

"A guy by the name of Douglas," I said, remembering what Mr. Zeeman had said.

Feldman scowled harder. "The vice president missed the papers, or was suspicious for some reason, we don't really know for sure quite what happened. There was a confrontation when Douglas got here and pulled a gun, and your dad tried to take it away from him. The agent walked in while they were struggling, and both men were shot. Douglas was bleeding profusely and he's in the hospital, refusing to say a thing except to accuse Steve Rakosi of attacking him."

I gasped in indignation, and Joanie said, "Dad wouldn't have shot anybody!"

"Unfortunately Rakosi took a bullet that skimmed along the side of his head. The doctors don't consider it to be a life-threatening injury, but he's been in and out of consciousness, and when he's come around he hasn't been entirely coherent. He can't remember any of what led up to the incident, and doesn't know where he put the incriminating papers we need to prove what was going on."

He paused and drew a deep breath. "Anyway, both Rakosi and Douglas needed immediate medical attention. But our agent didn't want to alert anyone in the apartment house that the incident had taken place. They suspected Douglas might have a partner. The agency wanted to keep him in the dark while they tried to get the evidence to make an arrest before he could run with the money he'd stolen."

"So instead of calling an ambulance to the front door and taking Mr. Rakosi and Douglas down in the elevator, they carried them down the fire escape," Jake said with satisfaction.

Aaron Feldman glared at him. "Are you going to shut up long enough for me to tell this or not?"

"Sorry," Jake said meekly.

"It was after dark, and almost everybody from the apartments was up the street chasing a fire truck, so nobody saw the agent come in. He decided not to be seen leaving, either, so they loaded an unmarked ambulance from the alley after going down the fire escape."

"So it happened *Thursday* night, not last night," I blurted, then felt my face get red when Feldman turned the glare in my direction. I finished what I'd started to say, though. "And then you came in here while I was asleep on the couch and took the pipe and the picture."

He gave me a funny look. "I'm not an investigative agent, but my brother-in-law is. He noticed how much Rakosi looks like me—or I look like him—so when Rakosi was hurt, they talked me into moving in over here to pretend to be him in case anyone came poking around before we recovered the papers. They even had the fake ID made up in case I had to go into the office and pretend to be him on the job for a day or so, or anybody got curious enough to search me. I was to stay here just to make it look like Rakosi was still here, and we hoped our beards and our size would fool anybody that didn't know your dad very well. Nobody could prove Douglas ever came here; nobody saw him, as far as anybody knew. We hoped if we kept him incommunicado in the hospital, his partner would surface and expose himself."

"So you were staying here, pretending to be Dad, and you left a pipe and a picture of a woman," I said, then clapped my hand over my mouth.

"When I came back to look for the papers again, I retrieved my pipe and saw I'd dropped a picture of my sister. Her little girl had stuck it in my coat pocket, and it apparently fell out when I had my jacket off. I didn't expect to find you kids here, so I backed off to decide how to tackle it without giving anything away. I came back, because we *have* to find those papers, and the sooner the better. Without them we can't bring charges against Douglas, and we probably can't keep him hidden in the hospital very much longer."

Joanie leaned forward earnestly. "But they told us Daddy wasn't in the hospital!"

"He's there under a false name, under police guard. The doctor thinks he'll remember what he did with the papers, sooner or later, but the longer it takes, the bigger the risk that Douglas's partner— we're pretty sure he and Zeeman are in it together— will take off. So I need to search this place again, more thoroughly."

"We've already looked every place we could think of for a clue," I said, and this time he didn't give me a dirty look. "Because of the blood."

"Are there a lot of papers?" Jake wanted to know. "A big bundle, or what?"

"We don't know. He never had a chance to tell us before he got in a tussle with Douglas over the gun. Zeeman—the president of the union—seemed suspicious of me. Maybe," Feldman admitted, "you kids being here helped convince him I was legit, but he knows papers are missing. Either I took them, or Douglas did. He has a lot at stake, and he may be dangerous if he comes back."

We all stared at one another for a long minute.

I swallowed audibly. "So what do we do, then?"

"*You* go home," Feldman said. "And I stall, hoping the papers turn up, or your dad remembers where they are, before Monday. It's not likely I could fool any of the people Steve really worked with into thinking I'm him. And Zeeman knows I'm not sick, so he'll expect me on the job on Monday, if he doesn't bolt himself before then. I think I got away with convincing Zeeman that I was Steve Rakosi, because he'd never seen your dad except the day they were introduced, apparently. But either way, he's in a dangerous situation until he locates those papers, and that makes *him* dangerous."

"So let's get going, then," Jake said, getting up. "Let's search this place again, top to bottom, for the papers."

"When can we go see my dad?" I asked.

"I don't know if you can," he said. "You'll probably have to wait until the whole matter is cleared up before it'll be safe for anybody to visit him."

So we searched again, in every crack, every drawer, under and behind everything movable.

We didn't find a thing.

13

Aaron Feldman slumped into Dad's chair and stared at us.

"Well, if your dad hid the papers here, he did a real good job of it. I don't know anywhere else to look."

Nobody had any suggestions. I wanted to go see Dad, but Feldman said absolutely not. He turned to me now and ordered, "Go ahead and pack up your stuff, and we'll call a cab to get you to the bus station."

"The only bus has already gone for today," Jake said cheerfully. "The next one's tomorrow morning."

"Oh, great. So I have to worry about you for another day." Feldman had been fairly civil while we were searching the apartment, but he was back to scowling again. "Pack everything except your pajamas and your toothbrushes, then, so you'll be ready." He swore softly under his breath.

Joanie looked at him sadly. "Why are you so grumpy? Why don't you like us?"

Exasperated, he scratched his head. "I don't know

you well enough to know if I like you or not. It's just that this is a dangerous situation, and it will be safer when you get out of here. The men involved in embezzling hundreds of thousands in union funds have a lot at stake. They don't want to be caught. If they're cornered, they may go so far as to shoot their way out, and they probably wouldn't care if some of their victims were kids. Nobody from this apartment can go to the hospital to see your dad because they may be watching us. We can't take a chance they'll follow us and find out we not only have Rakosi there but Douglas. If Zeeman realizes I'm an imposter, and I attempt to go to work at the union office on Monday, it's unlikely I can fool the people he was getting to know. Which might"—and he said this quite seriously—"end up with someone shooting me or running me over a cliff to stop whatever they think I'm up to."

"But he wouldn't think Vickie and I would be dangerous to them," Joanie reasoned. "We're just kids."

"Right, and kids make swell hostages," Feldman pointed out. "To shut up your dad, if they think he hasn't told anyone what's going on yet, or to cover themselves if they try to flee the country."

"Hostages?" I echoed. It gave me goose bumps. I like thrillers, either in books or on TV, but being part of a real live hostage situation didn't sound like anything I wanted to try.

Joanie bit her lip. "You mean, like . . . kidnapping us? Holding us around the neck with a gun pointed to our heads?"

"Close enough," Feldman said, and stood up. "I

don't see what else I can do here. I need to go talk to some people who know more about this business than I do. I'll be glad when this is over and I can go back to working on truck engines."

"What were you doing down there in the alley?" Jake wanted to know.

Feldman hesitated. "I hope you were the only ones watching me. I had your dad's keys, so I'd been checking out his car again. I went through it once, in case he left the papers in it somewhere, but when nothing turned up here, and Steve Rakosi woke up but still couldn't tell us anything, I was desperate enough to go over everything more thoroughly. Then Zeeman showed up, and I didn't want to face him out there and pretend to be still sick. I was hoping to avoid him altogether."

"How'd you know who he was?" Jake asked.

"His car had been described to me, and I had the license number. And the agency showed me snapshots of both Zeeman and Douglas. I figured I had a better chance of keeping up the masquerade if I tackled him here."

"How did Douglas get here?" Jake persisted. "Did he have a car, too?"

"The agency took care of it. It might spook Zeeman if he thinks his buddy just ran out on him, so the car's under cover." He started toward the door. "You should be all right here for now; I'll only be gone for an hour or so."

When he had gone Jake said, "Is it okay with you if I stick around? I mean, this is kind of fascinating."

"If you want to," I said, not admitting that I'd feel better if he did.

We went ahead and packed our suitcases as Feldman had told us to, and then when Joanie said she was hungry, we raided what was left in the kitchen. It wasn't all that much. I guessed Dad must have eaten most of his meals out instead of cooking.

"I hope somebody's going to take care of Clancy after we go home," Joanie said. "Feed him, anyway."

"There isn't much cat food left. Not enough for more than a couple of days at the most. I wonder if cats can eat dog food if they're hungry enough?"

"Probably enough to keep them from starving," Jake said, spreading peanut butter on crackers. "I'll get some more tuna if he needs it. I don't dare buy cat food in case my old man sees it. He'd have kittens himself if he knew I was paying to feed a cat."

We ate in silence after that, feeling kind of depressed. Not only was I not going to get to see Dad, but at the end of the long bus ride I would have to face Gram before Mom got home. I could imagine what that was going to be like.

"It'll be boring when you leave," Jake said, standing up when he finished eating. "Back to listening to my old man complain, and Magda and Harold yelling at each other, and Old Man Becker's cops-and-robbers shows. I think—"

We never got to hear what he thought. He took a step toward the sink and George got right under Jake's feet. Jake tripped and lurched toward the counter, grabbing for something to steady himself, and we all recoiled from the crash as the glass coffeemaker fell. It went over the edge of the counter, stretching out the cord until the weight of the pot unplugged it. The cord caught on the bag of coffee that had been sitting beside the pot, and over the edge that went, too.

I remember thinking that Gram would have chewed Dad's ear for having the coffee out beside the pot instead of put away in the cupboard. Gram insisted on putting everything out of sight, and Dad was just as great for having things where he expected to use them. Like coffee beside the pot and his razor on the edge of the sink and his coat over the back of the chair nearest the front door instead of in the closet. Mom had just groaned over such things, but they drove Gram wild.

The fresh-ground coffee smell flooded the kitchen as the contents of the sack poured out. When Jake stepped in it, his feet went out from under him and he sat down hard.

"You okay?" I asked uncertainly when he didn't get up right away.

George licked at his ear, and Jake finally moved, shoving him away. "Yeah. Cripes, what a mess. Watch it, Joanie, don't step in the glass. Where's the broom?"

I walked around the edge of the mess. "The vacuum would probably be easier, at least on the coffee. You pick up the bigger pieces of glass, Jake, and I'll get it."

When we plugged it in, though, it made a noise but it didn't suck up anything.

Jake frowned. "What kind of a crummy vacuum cleaner is this? It won't pick up even a grain."

Joanie scooted around the coffee grounds and broken glass and into the living room, taking George with her. I hoped she'd shut Clancy outside or put him in the bedroom. There wasn't any big hulla-baloo, so I guessed the cat and the dog weren't to-gether, anyway.

"Maybe the bag's full of dirt," I suggested. "Dad forgets to empty it sometimes."

I bent over to pop the catches open and reached for the bag.

And then my breath caught in my throat.

"I found them," I said shakily. "Look! It's the pa-pers Dad hid, isn't it?"

Jake, on his knees with a handful of glass shards, leaned over to look. "Sure looks like it. Here, put them on the table and we'll put the bag back in place and clean up the mess. Boy, Mr. Feldman will be pleased when he gets back, I guess."

Only when the knock came on the door, and Joanie eagerly ran to open it to tell Mr. Aaron Feld-man the good news, it wasn't the mechanic-turned-agent who shoved his way into the room at all.

It was Mr. Zeeman, and he had a very ugly look on his face.

I stood stock-still, thinking of those papers spread out on the kitchen table.

We'd sort of glanced at them, but they didn't re-ally mean anything to us, just a lot of figures and sig-natures in writing so bad we couldn't make most of them out.

Feldman had said he'd be back in an hour or so. Almost that much time had passed now. My heart was pounding. What would happen if he came back? Feldman didn't have a gun, and I didn't know if Zeeman did or not.

We had to stop Zeeman from getting the papers

and leaving with them. They were evidence that Dad had risked his life to get. But what could we do?

In the closed kitchen, George whined and scratched. This time I didn't tell him to shut up. I hoped he sounded intimidating enough to keep Zeeman out of there.

"Where's your father?" Zeeman demanded. He wasn't even pretending to be polite this time.

"He's in the h—"

I crashed into Joanie, having to shut her up quick, and spoke over what she'd begun to say. "He had to go out. He'll be home any minute."

Joanie rubbed her arm. "What did you do that for?"

"Sorry, I bumped her," Jake said, close behind me. "Why don't you sit down, sir, and wait for him? He shouldn't be long."

By this time it dawned on Joanie that she'd almost told the man Dad was in the hospital, which Zeeman might find kind of odd since he'd seen the man he thought was Steve Rakosi such a short time earlier. I hoped he couldn't read Joanie's face as well as I did.

I sure didn't read anything in *his* face, except that he seemed menacing. He didn't move to sit down, but towered over us. "You're here alone?"

"Except for me," Jake said. I couldn't tell if *he* was scared, but I was.

"You're sure Rakosi hasn't left town?"

"And left us behind?" I asked, trying to sound incredulous. "No, he should be back any minute."

"Well, I don't have time to sit and wait for him,"

Zeeman informed us. "I'm going to have to ask you to stay out of the way while I look around this apartment."

My breath caught in my throat. Where was Feldman? What were we supposed to do by ourselves?

"We can't let you do that!" Jake asserted. "Not while Mr. Rakosi is gone!"

"How do you propose to stop me?" Zeeman demanded. "Mr. Rakosi lied to me. He took some papers that don't belong to him, and I mean to have them back. If he's gone to dispose of them, that was a big mistake. If they're still here, I'll take them now and leave you kids alone."

I didn't know if Joanie caught the implied threat, but I did. If he didn't get his papers, he'd do something with Joanie and me, and maybe even with Jake. I tried not to think about *what*.

Jake suddenly spread his hands as if to indicate that he was giving up. "Okay. Look around. I don't think you'll find any missing papers, though."

Zeeman gave him a suspicious glare, then walked toward the desk and started pulling out drawers, shuffling through the papers that had been neatly stacked.

We stood silently, watching. I was hoping he'd be stalled long enough in here so he wouldn't have time to get to the kitchen before Aaron Feldman came back.

He finished with the desk, started knocking books out of the bookcase, then turned savagely to the couch and pulled out the cushions and threw them on the floor.

At the window, Clancy appeared. "Bring him in," I told Joanie, trying to send her a message with my eyes.

She looked startled, then went to get the cat. Zeeman raked us all with that unfriendly gaze, but he didn't see how the cat could be dangerous, so he didn't stop her.

And then, suddenly, we heard two shots. They were loud, as if in the next room. And sirens, police cars maybe, coming closer and closer.

Zeeman jerked, looking around. I wondered if his mouth had gone dry as mine. Feldman, where are you? I begged silently.

And then, like magic, Feldman was there. The door had been left ajar when Zeeman arrived, and Feldman shoved it open, then closed it behind him.

"Oh, Mr. Zeeman. I didn't expect you back so soon," he said, as if he hadn't become aware of the tension in the room.

Behind his voice, the shrilling of the siren swelled to an earsplitting level, then ceased. There was another shot.

"What the heck's going on?" Jake demanded. "Are the cops *here*?"

"Who are they shooting at?" Joanie wanted to know, her eyes wide as she clutched Clancy against her chest.

I wasn't expecting what happened next. Mr. Zeeman took two quick steps toward me and wrapped an arm around my neck, jerking me backward against him. I could smell cigars and after-shave. And fear. The kind of sweat you get when you're afraid. I didn't know if it was his or mine.

"If I have to leave without the papers," Zeeman said very softly, "she goes with me. I don't guarantee you'll get her back."

For seconds—it seemed much longer—we stood there as if someone had pushed the Pause button on the VCR remote control. Nobody moved. I couldn't breathe, and my chest hurt.

I had to do something, and quickly, but what? If he made me leave with him, would I ever get loose?

Behind me, just to the side, George scratched and whined on the other side of the door. Immediately, Clancy stiffened in Joanie's arms, his eyes going wide in alarm.

I failed the first time I tried to speak, and then I croaked, "Put Clancy down, Joanie."

She didn't understand, but for the second time in her life she did what she was told without asking any questions. She lowered her arms and let the cat slide to the floor.

At the same time, I twisted to reach the doorknob that was only a foot away, and opened the kitchen door.

Everybody but Zeeman realized what was coming. George came bounding free, torn between Clancy and the enemy whose pants he'd torn earlier. Mr. Zeeman was closer, and he couldn't leap to the top of the bookcase the way Clancy did. George sank his teeth into Mr. Zeeman's left leg.

It got a little crazy for the next minute or two. I didn't see it all right then, I just replayed it in my mind later.

Jake dove for the phone. I didn't have to be told he was dialing 911 for the cops.

Joanie cried out and stumbled out of the way. As soon as Zeeman's arm fell away from my neck, I dove sideways, through the doorway into the kitchen. And Aaron Feldman, maybe spurred on by what sounded like rescue as the sirens screamed and the shots rang out again, landed a real haymaker on Mr. Zeeman's jaw.

Jake yelled into the phone, Joanie was too scared even to cry, and the two men rolled on the floor while I tried to drag George away when he mistook Feldman for his original target.

Both men were cursing and slugging each other. When George jerked away from me and luckily found Mr. Zeeman again, though, the fight began to go out of our enemy.

"For pete's sake," Feldman gasped, "get hold of that dog!"

When Jake came to help me, we finally got George under control.

The sirens and gunshots ceased. A moment later, while we were all puffing and trying to restart our hearts, Jake said, "The cops are on their way." At that moment Mr. Becker eased open the door and put his head around the edge of it.

"Is . . . is everything all right in here?" he asked uncertainly. "I thought I heard . . . oh." He stared at Zeeman, flat on the floor with Feldman sitting on him. "Oh, I was afraid my TV had disturbed you again. It came on so loud, and when I went to turn down the volume the knob fell off and rolled under the couch, and I couldn't . . ." He blinked, inspecting our practically wrecked room. "Oh," he said again, and withdrew.

We all breathed loudly, painfully. When Zeeman twisted convulsively in an attempt to break free, Feldman bounced on him, squashing the air out. That sounded painful, too.

In only a few minutes we heard sirens again, only this time they were real, not on TV.

Zeeman suddenly renewed his struggle, and he might have escaped even then if he hadn't been both held down by a heavier man and intimidated by the dog we held on his leash only a foot from his head. Clearly George would have been only too glad to attack his enemy again if Jake and I hadn't held him off.

I was sure glad when the police got there. My arms felt as if I'd been stretched out on a medieval torture rack when Jake finally dragged the bulldog back to Magda's apartment. He shut him up there while Harold yelled questions and wanted to know who was going to pay for the damage George and the rest of us had done to his apartment.

Aaron Feldman had to explain a few things to the cops before they checked in for instructions and then put handcuffs on Zeeman. I saw his face as they led him away—out the front way, with practically everybody in the apartment house watching, looking almost as bug-eyed as George—and I was sure glad he hadn't been able to escape with me as his hostage.

The last police officer paused in the doorway to look back at us. "We had a call from up in Washington State about a couple of runaways. Are you them, by any chance?"

"Are you going to arrest us?" Joanie asked, going big-eyed again.

He sighed. "If we arrested all the runaways in this country, we wouldn't have time to fight crime. Can we report to the party that called that you're in charge of them, sir?"

"Me?" Feldman said, sounding startled, and then he nodded. "Yeah, tell the family they'll be home soon. I'll be putting them back on the bus as soon as I can."

When they were all gone, Feldman swiped a hand through his hair and sighed, and I finally got a chance to speak. "We found the papers," I said.

Feldman, who had been dejectedly looking at the demolished room and at his garments, torn where George had managed to get a tooth-hold, froze.

"You what?" he said.

"We found the papers. They were in the vacuum cleaner, and they're on the kitchen table."

And that was really the end of it. Well, it was the end as far as Joanie and I were concerned.

We got loaded on the bus the next morning and sent home, and meeting Gram was even worse than I'd expected. She'd been upset, but worried more about how Mom would react than about us, I think. She was afraid to contact Mom and tell her what had happened until she knew for sure we were okay, and then she played down the whole thing as one of my immature and inconsiderate pranks. Not her fault, of course.

Gram never settles for pointing out a mistake or explaining how stupid somebody is if she can repeat it a dozen times. We had four days of it before Mom got home. I was ready to run away again, but somehow I wasn't quite brave enough to do it.

Before we left San Sebastian they'd let us visit Dad in the hospital, so we knew he was getting better. He was glad to see us, but he bawled me out.

"I can't believe what you did, Vickie. Running away, coming down here without asking either me or your mother if it was all right."

"You don't know how bad it was with Gram," I began, but he cut me off.

"I was in the middle of a very dangerous situation, and you could easily have been caught up in it. If you'd walked in when I was fighting for control of that gun, you could have been shot as easily as I was. You could have been killed. *I* could have been killed trying to protect you."

"Gram was—", I said desperately, but he talked right over top of me.

"If you ever do such a stupid thing again I'll see to it you don't sit down for a week. I don't care *how* old you are, you acted in a completely irresponsible, inconsiderate manner and the consequences could have been terrible for a lot of people."

"I was only trying to help," I protested, finally getting in a whole sentence, but he didn't accept that, either.

"You knew perfectly well that none of the adults in the family would have given you permission to leave home, so you just did it on your own, without thinking how upset your mom would be, or what kind of trouble you might get into. I'm ashamed of you, Vickie. I planned to have you come down for part of the summer, that's why I got a bed to put in the spare room, but not this way. Not defying your grandmother. I know she's a pain, but Mom left her in charge of you. You can't overrule what Mom's decided."

My mouth moved, but nothing came out. I couldn't think what to say. Dad wasn't having that problem, though.

"Your grandmother's right. You don't *think*. All you consider is what *you* want, and that's not good enough. It's a very immature attitude."

Behind us, Mr. Feldman cleared his throat. "They did find the missing papers, though. Plenty of evidence, the authorities think, to put our friends in jail for a long time. And the kids kept their heads pretty well, all things considered."

Dad grunted. "I'd expect any kid of mine to keep her head. And I'm relieved it turned out all right. But you have to understand, Vickie, that you can't do anything like this again, ever."

I nodded meekly. "Okay," I agreed.

Feldman cleared his throat again. "I'm putting the kids on the next bus. What do you want to do about the cat?"

"We could take him home with us," Joanie suggested eagerly.

"I don't think they'd allow you to take him on the bus," Dad said, sounding less mad by now. "Maybe you can get that kid from upstairs to feed him until I get out of here. What's his name? Jake? Your mom's not going to accept Clancy as long as Gram is there, you know."

He saw Joanie's disappointment. "I'm sorry, honey. It's lonesome by myself, but I'm unemployed again, so unless I can work out something else I may not even be able to keep him myself."

Actually, I was kind of glad to get out of his hospital room and head for home. He hadn't raised a hand to me, but I felt as if I were stinging all over.

Before we caught the bus, Aaron Feldman took us out for pizza, and Magda came home and said she didn't mind that we'd eaten all her cookies. Jake promised he'd keep track of Dad and Clancy and George and Magda and let us know how they all were.

Mom called the hospital as soon as she got home. She went in the bedroom and closed the door, so I couldn't hear what she and Dad talked about.

When she came out, though, she announced in a calm voice that even Gram didn't argue with, "Steve's going to have to recuperate for a few weeks when they release him from the hospital. And of course his job's gone. I heard that his old boss's son-in-law isn't working out too well. Maybe there's a chance Dad can work in Washington again; he wants to be closer to the kids. And he suggested that I refinance the house; we have quite a bit of equity, and he thinks we might be able to lower the payments enough so I can handle them better."

I sucked in a breath, waiting for the punch line, even praying for it. And I got the one I wanted.

"In the meantime, I told him he could come back home, at least until he's able to work again."

Gram didn't say anything to that, not then. The next morning, though, she had an announcement of her own.

"I've decided to go to Montana to visit my cousin Rachel for the summer. If I like it there, and you can manage the house payments on your own, I may stay. She's asked me to share *her* house, and she doesn't have any children."

I thought Mom might try to argue her out of going, maybe just to be polite, but she didn't. She only smiled. "I think Mrs. Blade, across the street, would keep an eye on the kids again, the way she used to before. She said maybe Vickie could help with her little ones in exchange. And I think you and Cousin Rachel would get along fine with that arrangement, Mother."

And I knew *we* would.

Mom wasn't finished, though. "You know, Vickie, you have to be punished for running away, and dragging Joanie with you. It was inexcusable to do something you knew I wouldn't have allowed."

I swallowed, waiting.

"I think it would be fair if you were grounded for the next month," Mom said, sounding firmer than I could ever remember.

"Dad said she deserved to be grounded for all summer," Joanie piped up. I had to struggle to keep from smacking her. My face felt as if it were on fire.

Gram had to stick in her two cents worth, naturally. "That's the most sensible thing I ever heard Steve say," she contributed.

To my horror, Mom seemed to be seriously considering it. "For now, let's say it's *at least* a month. When your father comes, we'll decide together if that's enough."

And just like I thought, Joanie got off without any punishment at all. It was *my* fault, not hers.

It was a relief when they finally stopped talking about it. And by the time Dad got home, nobody seemed to remember that they'd considered keeping me under house arrest for the whole summer, so it only lasted until two weeks after school was out.

I felt good enough about everything by then so that I even helped Joanie make a fancy lacy birthday card for Gram.

I think, if she's in Missoula instead of in Marysville, I may even write her a letter once in a while. I'd like her to know I haven't done anything really stupid for at least a month.

I may even read what she writes back. Now and then she does say something sensible, after all, like how pretty Montana is.

Besides, even if she does keep saying, "Think of the consequences, Victoria" (in her letters, too!), she does make terrific cookies. She might send us some for Christmas.

Maybe by then Dad will be home to stay.